If You Can't Be Good,
Be Good at It

Hook Up or Break Up

If You Can't Be Good, Be Good at It

KENDALL ADAMS

HarperTempest
An Imprint of HarperCollins*Publishers*
A PARACHUTE PRESS BOOK

HarperTempest is an imprint of HarperCollins Publishers.

If You Can't Be Good, Be Good at It
Copyright © 2006 by Parachute Publishing, LLC

Library of Congress Catalog Card Number: 2006920318
ISBN-10: 0-06-088564-5 — ISBN-13: 978-0-06-088564-9

Typography by Sasha Illingworth

First HarperTempest edition, 2006

If You Can't Be Good, Be Good at It

one

"Layla Sunrise Carter! What the heck are you doing?" My best friend, Cara Matz, leaned on the locker next to mine and stared me down. "Explain yourself!"

"Okay, first of all, could we refrain from uttering my middle name in public?" I asked. I shoved my AP European History text into my locker and slammed the door shut. "I mean, harpoon my social life, why don't you?"

"Uh, sorry, but I think you've already done that yourself," Cara said, her pale blue eyes open wide. "Why did you break up with Josh? I thought you liked him."

"Yes. *Liked*. As in past tense," I said. "Let's go to lunch already. I'm starving."

I stepped around her and started down the crowded hallway to the cafeteria. I knew from experience that Cara was not going to be deterred so easily. The girl wanted to see me in a serious relationship more than she wanted to wake up one day with her corkscrew-curly blond hair spontaneously straightened—and she'd wanted *that* since kindergarten. But at least I could grab a bagel and eat while she ranted. For some reason, dumping a guy always made me hungry.

"I mean, two weeks ago we're on a double date and everything is fine. You're feeding each other French fries, you're laughing at all his jokes, and then you just callously break up with him this morning in study hall. Without even consulting me!" Cara sighed as we shoved our way into the cafeteria. "He and Mike totally got along, too. It could have been perfect."

Ah, Mike. The real reason behind Cara's eagerness to see me tied down. Mike and Cara had been going out since freshman year. They were nauseatingly cute together and Cara was beyond happy with him. I suppose I couldn't blame her for wanting to see me that happy, too, but I had yet to find a guy I wanted to hang out with for more than three dates. After that they all just became boring. Or annoying. Or both.

"Sorry. You are just gonna have to remain a twosome for a little while longer," I said with a shrug.

"But I really wanted a foursome," Cara complained.

A couple of sophomore girls looked at her in a shocked way as they walked past. Cara flushed.

"Not in a sexual way!" she shouted after them. "Great. Now everyone's gonna think I have an orgy fetish," Cara said, throwing her hands up.

"Who cares? They're sophomores," I said. I wrapped my arm around her as we joined the lunch line. "Josh and I were just not meant to be, okay? Sheesh. You're more depressed about this than I am."

"Yeah. What's that about?" Cara asked, handing me a tray and taking one for herself.

I shrugged. "I'm just good at moving on. In fact, could we move on from this conversation already?"

"Uh, hardly," she said, grabbing a plain bagel for herself and an everything bagel for me. "I want to know what happened. What was wrong with this one? Chewed with his mouth open? Strange body odor? Did he call you too often? Not enough? Wear too much blue?"

I paused in front of the fruit basket. "God. You make me sound so shallow."

"I'm sorry. No. Those were all very good breakup reasons at the time," she said. "And I'm sure you have a very good reason now unless you jumped to another one of your crazy conclusions." She grabbed an apple and pulled out her wallet. "So, what was it?"

I winced. This was not going to sound good in the current context.

"Model airplanes?" I said.

Cara looked at me like, *Come on, already!* "Please tell me you're kidding. You dumped Josh Thorenson because he has a *hobby*? Are you on drugs?"

I looked around. Cara really had to work on that volume problem of hers. "Yes. Yes, I'm on drugs, Cara. Are you trying to get me expelled?"

She rolled her eyes and we paid for our lunches. As we made our way to our usual table, I tried not to glance toward Josh's. I hoped he wasn't upset and moping, but if he was, I didn't want to see it. Clean break. That was what it was all about. Don't get emotionally involved too quickly.

Cara dropped her tray, sat down, and picked up right where we had left off.

"Okay, on a scale of one to ten, one being Deke 'the Geek' Kostopolis and ten being, of course, Drew Sullivan, you rated Josh a seven!"

She had a point. Not many people had come closer to Drew-level hotness. It had been two years since Drew Sullivan had graduated from Kensington High School and I still compared every guy I met to him—even though we had never actually spoken. Who needed to talk to the guy when he had those beautiful hazel eyes and that longish, messy brown hair that only he could pull off without looking like a reject from the grunge era? Then there was the motorcycle. And the artistic talent. Hot, artsy boy on a bike? Didn't get much better than that. A girl could fantasize about Drew Sullivan for days.

"Hello? I'm over here," Cara said, waving her hand in front of my face until I snapped to. "What was wrong with Josh?"

"Cara, you don't understand. Yesterday I went over to Josh's house and there were a zillion model airplanes hanging from the ceiling in his room," I said, shaking up my iced tea. "So I'm like, okay, it's a motif. Fine. I can handle

4

that. But then the dining room table was covered with newspaper and there were five different airplanes in various stages of put-togetherness."

Cara scoffed. "That is so not a word."

"He had model airplane books and model airplane magazines and, get this, a huge poster of Leonardo DiCaprio from *The Aviator* inside his closet door," I told her with all the gravity the statement merited.

"You're kidding."

"I am *so* not. By now I'm seriously questioning his sexuality, right? I mean, Leo? *Inside* the closet? Hello, subtext!"

Cara laughed.

"But *then* he starts kissing me and he's clearly into it, so I'm thinking okay, maybe he *does* swing our way, until he moves the action to the bed and you'll never believe what I saw there."

Cara's eyes widened. She was riveted. "What?"

"Airplane sheets. The guy has *airplane sheets*. Sexually ambiguous with the sheets of a kindergartner? That's where I draw the line."

Cara laughed again. "So it actually *wasn't* about the model airplanes."

I blinked. "No. I guess not." Apparently I wasn't quite so shallow.

"Okay. So who's next?" Cara asked, popping a piece of bagel into her mouth.

Ouch. I knew I dated around a lot, but she didn't have to make it sound so . . . I don't know . . . expected.

"What am I, a revolving door?" I asked.

Cara turned pink and took a sip of her water to make the bagel go down easier.

"You know that's not what I meant," she said, once she'd finally swallowed. "I just want you to fall in love already."

"Why? Why is it *so* important that I fall in love?" I asked, trying to keep my tone light.

"Because I think you'd like having a boyfriend," Cara said. "And you deserve one. A good one. Someone who'll buy you little presents and drive you to school . . ."

"I have you for that," I pointed out with a smirk.

Cara narrowed her eyes. "Maybe I should stop driving you. Then you'll have to get a boyfriend."

I pushed my long, chestnut brown hair over one shoulder. "I've got two feet that work," I said blithely.

"Ha-ha," Cara said, pulling out a notebook and pen. "That's it. I'm making a list."

"A list? Of what?" I asked, munching on my bagel.

"Eligible bachelors," she said. "Ones you haven't dated."

"Good luck with that," I said, rolling my eyes. I hadn't been *that* busy over the past few years, but Kensington was a small school in a small New York town slightly north of the city. We only had so many worthy guys to go around. I glanced at my watch and gathered my things. "I gotta go."

"What? Why? You're not gonna help?" she asked, clearly bummed.

"I don't know, Cara, chasing guys isn't really my thing.

I like it when they come to me," I said. "If it's gonna happen, it's gonna happen."

Cara sighed. "All right, fine. But can I make the list anyway?"

The girl did love her lists. Probably why she got a perfect score on her verbal SAT. For two straight years she *lived* for those vocab lists.

"Knock yourself out," I said, hoisting my fringed messenger bag over my shoulder, and grabbing my bagel and iced tea. "Meanwhile, I'll be in the library researching a viewpoint piece on the U.S. Patriot Act for next week's *Reporter*. Who's the smarty now?"

Cara and I were co-editors of the school newspaper, *The Reporter*, and sometimes we let ourselves get competitive with our pieces.

"Yeah. You keep telling yourself that."

Cara waved me off, returning her attention to the list. She was such a romantic. Sometimes I wished I was more like her—that I could even wrap my brain around the idea of having a serious boyfriend—but ever since my parents' seriously messy divorce, I had been sort of doubtful about the whole long-term relationship thing. And besides, I was only seventeen. Why would I want to tie myself down when I should be living it up?

I was almost to the cafeteria doors when I heard someone calling my name.

"Layla! Hey, Layla! Wait up!"

I stopped by the drink machines near the door and turned. Nate Henry, super hoop star and fellow psych-elective student, was jogging to catch up with me. Never in my life had I talked to this guy. Not once. We didn't exactly circulate in the same, well, circles. Nate was cute and all, with his short, wavy blond hair and cornflower blue eyes, but he was way too J.Crew for my tastes. All argyle sweaters and pristine white T-shirts. I liked my guys a little . . . dirtier.

Of course, half the girls in school were salivating to wear his varsity jacket. To all the jocks and social butterflies and anyone who aspired to be a jock or a social butterfly, he was the hottest of the hot.

"Man, you walk fast," he said, catching his breath.

"What's up?" I asked.

Nate blinked and averted his eyes. "Oh. I, uh . . ." He shifted his weight from foot to foot. "Good question! What *is* up?"

I raised my eyebrows. This was intriguing. He had come running after me and he had nothing to say. Could this be, perhaps, a prelude to an ask-out? Me and Nate Henry. Everyone would just die. Seriously. The halls would be littered with carcasses.

I found myself studying Nate for the first time. Could I go there?

"I was wondering if you did the psych reading," he blurted finally.

"Uh-huh," I told him.

He really was kind of cute. If I could just mess up his hair a little and maybe untuck that shirt . . .

"Cool . . ." he said, pressing one fist into the other palm.

He was exhibiting all the classic symptoms. Goofy

greeting? Check. Lame conversational topic? Check. Fidgeting? Check. It was kind of charming. I would have thought with his star power and half the school wanting his bod, he'd be a cocky jerk, but he was practically sweating. But then I remembered that even though he's super popular, he'd never had a serious girlfriend. Hmmm . . .

"I thought that stuff about the whole codependent relationship thing was kind of cool, you know?" Nate said. He reached out to rest an arm on a drink machine all casually . . . and missed. He stumbled, almost crashing sideways into the wall, but caught himself on the machine and turned beet red.

"Are you okay?" I asked, grinning.

"Yeah. Sure! I . . . uh. . . ."

Okay. We had to end this before someone got hurt. I flipped my hair over my shoulder and tilted my head.

"Nate, is there . . . I don't know, something else you wanted?" I asked.

"Right! Yeah, well, I . . . I heard about you and Josh," he said. "I'm really sorry."

"Yeah?"

"Yeah. And I was just sort of wondering if you might want to go out with me sometime," he said quickly. "Like, maybe tonight? To a movie?"

Right. So I had two choices. I could either say yes and reveal the fact that I was planless that evening, or I could tell him I was busy and then stay home by myself watching *Made* all night long. And really, what kind of life was that? Option A it was.

"Sure," I said. "Give me a call later. I'm in the book."

"Yeah? Great. That's great," he said, suddenly psyched. "I'll call you after practice."

"I'll talk to you then," I assured him.

I waited for him to bound back to his table like a happy puppy before casually strolling over to where Cara was still sitting.

"Hey," I said to Cara.

She glanced up, startled. "You're back! Why are you grinning like that?"

"Oh, because Nate Henry just asked me out," I said nonchalantly.

"Nate Henry?" she said with a gasp. "No way! Nate—"

I dropped down into the chair next to hers and slapped my hand over her mouth before she could go all supersonic again.

"Shhh! Calm down," I said, even though my own heart was skipping happily. Who knew that Nate Henry could have that kind of effect on me? One conversation and already I could kind of see what all the other girls saw in him. It was very rare that a guy that hot was also that sweet.

"Omigod, Layla. Nate Henry is the single most eligible bachelor in school," she said, producing her list. "Look!"

Sure enough, Nate was right on top of her, so far, very short list.

"It's fate," she said.

I smiled slowly. Maybe it *was* fate.

"Okay, stop channeling my mother," I said. If there was

anyone who was all about fate and destiny and star signs, it was Mom. "Want to come over after school to help me pick out something to wear? Hey! I'll even let you do my hair."

"My straightening iron and I will be there," Cara replied with a grin. "We wouldn't miss it for the world."

two

Six hours later, my hair was perfectly stick-straight and Nate was opening the door of his silver Prius for me. A seventeen-year-old gentleman. Who knew it was possible?

"My mom would love this car," I said as he climbed in behind the wheel. "She's all about the environment."

"Ex-hippy?" he asked.

"Try current. Current, active, and cardholding."

Nate checked out my outfit: knee-high boots, skinny jeans, and a graphic tee topped with a fitted blazer. "I never pictured you as the tree-hugging type."

"I'm not," I replied. "Not really. I mean, I'm all for recycling, but other than that I don't have much in common with my mother. I want to be a lawyer. She burst a few blood vessels when I told her that one. May as well have said, 'Mom? I'm gonna be a stripper!'"

Nate blushed at the mention of the word *stripper*. Aw. He really was just too cute.

"Sorry. Did I embarrass you?" I teased.

"No! Not at all," Nate said, clearing his throat and checking the mirrors about two dozen times before pulling out onto the street. "So . . . what do you want to see?"

"I don't know. I'm up for anything," I said. As always. "What about you? Are you an action flick kind of guy, or are you down for something classic?"

"I could go for classic," he said.

I smiled and sat back. "I was hoping you'd say that."

By the end of *Rebel Without a Cause*, I was transfixed, but not by the movie. I couldn't stop staring at Nate. When I'd suggested the throwback movie house, I had expected him to grumble about it or just grin and bear it, but he was totally into the flick. He had even mouthed a few of the lines along the way, as if he'd seen the movie a million times before. How many super jocks could say that? Nate Henry was a lot more interesting than I'd given him credit for.

Plus his profile was totally gorgeous.

The lights came up and I blinked my way out of my trance. Nate turned to me and I instantly looked at the screen, hoping he hadn't caught me staring.

"Did you like it?" he asked, taking my soda cup and the half-empty bucket of popcorn as he stood.

"Loved it," I replied. "You?"

"Are you kidding? That's one of my favorite movies of all time, but I've never seen it on the big screen," he said. "Thanks for thinking of it."

I grinned. "No problem."

Nate stepped out into the aisle and let me walk ahead of him into the lobby.

"So, where to next?" Nate asked as we slipped into our jackets with the rest of the movie-goers. I slid over next to the wall to let an elderly couple pass.

"I could definitely eat," I said. "Why don't we hit Johnny's?"

A shadow of doubt crossed Nate's face and instantly my insides squirmed. Johnny's was a burger place in town where all the kids from school hung out. Did he, for some reason, not want to be seen with me?

"What?" I asked.

"I don't know. Everyone's gonna be there," he said.

Bingo. Mr. Big Man on Campus could not be seen with Ms. Couldn't Care Less What You Think of Me. I knew there was a flaw in there somewhere.

"Nate, why did you ask me out?" I asked point-blank. I had never been much for game playing.

Nate blinked, clearly taken aback. "What? What do you mean?"

"I mean why did you—a guy who can have any girl in the school—ask *me* out?" I said.

Please don't let it be because you heard I hook up a lot, I thought desperately. *Please do not turn out to be that kind of guy.*

14

Nate scoffed. "I can't have any girl in the school," he said, flushing.

"Are you trying to be modest, or are you really that clueless?" I said, my body temperature rising. "They all want you! The cheerleaders, the volleyball players, the fashion victims. All the most gorgeous, popular, cookie-cutter girls in the school."

"Well, maybe *I* don't want *them*," Nate blurted, his ears turning bright red. "Why are you so mad all of a sudden?"

"Nothing. Forget it," I said. "If you don't want to be seen with me, that's fine."

I turned toward the door, but Nate grabbed my arm. "Wait. Is that what this is about? Johnny's? Layla, the only reason I didn't want to go there was because I wanted to be alone with you, you know, to talk or whatever. If we go to Johnny's everyone's gonna be all over us. I don't know about you, but that's not really a date to me."

My heart warmed and I turned to face him. His blue eyes were open and honest and totally sincere.

"Really?" I said.

"Yeah," he replied, releasing his grip. "And as for the most gorgeous girls in the school, I thought I was out with one of them."

Whoa. Step back. We have a winner! I couldn't have stopped grinning if someone had stepped on my foot with a stiletto.

"Well, you are," I said, flicking my hair over my shoulder nonchalantly.

Nate grinned back. "You don't have any kind of

confidence problems, do you?"

"Not really," I answered.

"I like that."

He reached out and took my hand. His was soft and warm and fit perfectly around mine. Suddenly I felt tingly all over. Never felt *that* with Josh Thorensen.

"Now can we go someplace quiet and just . . . talk?" he asked.

I rolled my eyes playfully and ducked into the crook of his arm. "If you *insist*."

three

"You *still* haven't kissed him?" Cara blurted, staring at me in the girls' room mirror. "What, does he have perpetually bad breath or something?"

"Hardly." In fact, Nate's breath was always minty fresh—from a distance anyway.

It was Monday morning, three weeks after my first date with Nate. Since then, we had gone out on two more perfect dates, then hung out all weekend long, and he had yet to become annoying *or* boring. In fact, he had only turned out to be more sweet, more cool, and, if possible, more handsome, than I originally thought. But yes, it was true. He had yet to kiss me.

"Then I don't get it," Cara said.

"Hey, it's not like I don't want to. I mean, have you *seen* those lips?" I said, smoothing on a touch of strawberry gloss. "It's just, he hasn't made a move and I don't want to, like, jump him and scare him off or something. I don't want to ruin it."

"Uh-oh," Cara said, shaking her head. "You've got it bad."

"I do not!"

"Yes, you do! You *so* do!" Cara cried. "Omigod, this could be the one. Nate Henry could be your ultimate high school romance. Who knew?"

"Crazy, huh?" I giggled. I couldn't help it. Nate had turned me into a giggler. Me. Even thinking about the sweet way he'd kissed me on the cheek the night before made me shiver in a way a thousand lip kisses with other guys never had.

"I have literally never seen you like this," Cara said. She pulled out her own tube of lip balm and sang as she reapplied. *"Layla has a boyfriend, Layla has a boyfriend."*

Normally I would have smacked her upside the head, but instead I just sighed. "You know, I think I actually do."

"And just in time for Valentine's Day!" Cara announced.

"How *cheesy* is this?" I said, rolling my eyes.

Cara turned to me and smiled. "Actually, I think it's the perfect amount of cheesy."

Just then the door to the girls' room whooshed open and in walked Debra Jack and Hannah DeSalvo. They looked us up and down like we were mildew.

Now, I have nothing against cheerleaders, per se, except when they use their perkiness for evil. Which these girls lived to do. To the guys on the varsity teams Debra and Hannah were perfectly sweet and attentive, but to anyone who was not in their group (insert Cara and me here) they were total bitches.

"Did you hear about Nate and Jenny?" Debra began.

Cara and I looked at one another. My heart pretty much stopped.

"No!" Hannah said dramatically. "Are they together now?"

"Looks that way. They were totally hanging out at my party after the game on Saturday, and he was, like, all over her." She glanced at me in the mirror and smirked.

My heart thudded extra hard, but thankfully, I was able to keep my face impassive. After all, I knew she was lying. Nate had actually hung out with me after his game on Saturday. Plus there was no way Nate would ever go for Jenny "I have one functioning brain cell" Morrison behind my back. I knew where I stood.

"Oh, very subtle, Debra," I said, crossing my arms over my chest. "Did you learn that tactic at charm school?"

"Don't be all defensive, Layla," Hannah said, dusting some powder on her crooked nose. "It's not our fault Nate came to his senses and decided he could do better than the school slut."

She may as well have slapped me across the face. "What did you say to me?"

Debra sighed, snapped her compact closed, and tossed it in her bag. "If you can't take it, Layla, try not dishing it out to every guy in school."

For once in my life, I was rendered completely speechless.

"Who the hell do you think you are?" Cara said, stepping up to them. "You don't know anything about her."

Glad someone was able to find her tongue.

"Only that she keeps the Trojan company in business," Debra said, causing Hannah to snort a laugh. "Come on, Hannah," Debra said over her shoulder. "Let's go."

Then, with one more derisive glance back at me, they trailed by us out the door.

"Yeah! You'd *better* go!" Cara shouted after them.

I turned and leaned against the sink, feeling sick. "Did they really just say that to me?" I asked.

"Come on, Layla. They don't know what they're talking about," Cara said.

"Of course they don't! I don't sleep with every guy I date!"

"I know you don't," Cara said. "Debra's been in love with Nate since the fifth grade and he's never even looked at her. She's just jealous. Don't let them get to you."

I took a deep breath and groaned. "I'm not," I said. "I'm not. I just wish I had said something. God, I hate it when I don't have a comeback."

"That's why you've got me," Cara said, rubbing my back. "And when I don't have one, you always do."

"True," I said.

Cara's eyes were mischievous when they met mine in the mirror.

"Hey. Don't worry about it," she said. "Dating Nate is the best revenge."

I stood up straight and smiled back. She did have a point.

Thankfully, my first class was Spanish, where we were supposed to finish watching *The Motorcycle Diaries*. There was no way I would have been able to pay attention in an actual class just then. Thank goodness for Che Guevera and his poignant life story. The room would be dark and Mrs. Melendez would be riveted, so I fully intended to settle down for a forty-minute brood and catnap.

I leaned forward in my seat and rested my head in my hands as I waited for Mrs. Melendez to turn off the lights. If Debra and Hannah had decided I was a trashy slut, and they were part of Nate's clique of superiority, did that mean that he thought the same thing? Had he heard those rumors as well? Probably, if Debra had anything to say about it.

Damn, I wished I had said something to her. *Anything*. Maybe I should spend the next forty minutes formulating the perfect comeback so that I'd have it ready for the next time.

"Class, before I start the film, we have a new student I would like to introduce," Mrs. Melendez announced. "Everyone, this is Ian Cramer."

" 'Ello."

Well, that got my attention. A British accent in the middle of New York State? We weren't that far away from New York City but you still didn't hear exotic accents every day.

I glanced up and time stood still. At the front of the room was one seriously gorgeous bit of Yorkshire pudding.

He was tall and broad with dark brown skin, nearly black eyes, and dreadlocks that were tied back with a leather cord. His jeans, boots, and orange sweater were molded on a killer bod.

"Would anyone like to volunteer to help Ian get caught up in the class?"

Every female hand in the room shot up, including mine. Hey, the guy was a supermodel. It was sheer instinct.

"Layla. Good. Thank you," Mrs. Melendez said. I smiled triumphantly as every other girl in the room shot me unabashed looks of envy. "Ian, why don't you take the seat behind Layla's?" Mrs. Melendez suggested, pointing.

Ian's dark eyes fell on me and he smiled. It was a smile that could have made any woman on the planet melt instantly.

"With pleasure," he said in that killer accent.

He strode over to the empty seat behind mine and sat down.

"Taking pity on the tall, dark, and mysterious foreigner. Very altruistic of you," he whispered, leaning forward so that I could feel his warm breath on my neck.

"What can I say? I'm a sucker for clichés," I replied.

See? I *can* drop comebacks sometimes!

I turned slightly to face him. His lips were inches from mine and the air between us sizzled. Pheromones. Had to be. Really strong pheromones.

"Why don't we meet up in the library after school today?" I suggested. "I have a quick meeting, but I should be there by, like, three-fifteen. We can go over the book together and see where you are."

"Quarter past three," Ian said. "It's a date."

"In your dreams," I replied with a smile.

Dating Ian was out of the question. After all, I was dating Nate.

But tell that to my sweating palms and my skipping heart. Why did he have to be so damned hot? And so damned exotic? And why did I have to be such a sucker for both?

Nate was waiting for me by my locker after eighth period. His face completely lit up when he saw me coming. Sigh. A girl could get used to that.

"Hey," I said casually, starting in on my combination.

"Hi."

He shoved his hand into the front pocket of his jeans and leaned against the row of lockers. This boy could seriously be in an Abercrombie ad.

"So, we kind of saw a lot of each other this weekend," he said.

"Uh, every day?" I said. "Yeah, that's kind of a lot."

He leaned in closer and lowered his voice. "Guess that's why I missed you so much today."

It took serious effort to keep from shivering visibly on that one.

"You saw me in psych," I reminded him.

"Riiiight. Definitely not enough."

He reached out and hooked his pinky around mine. My heart thumped and I turned to him. He was looking at me with heavy-lidded "I want you" eyes.

Oh. My. God. Was this it? Was he finally going to kiss me? Had I used a mint after my daily everything bagel?

His eyes started to close. He inched closer to me. I tilted my head and tried not to grin. This *was* it! Finally! Yes!

"Hey, Nate!"

He sprang back, slamming into Peyton Christopher, whose locker was a few down from mine. Our lips had never even made it close. We both turned around to see Debra Jack shouting at him from the gym door.

"Coach wants you!" she practically sang.

Bitch. Big, fat, peroxided bitch.

"Uh, okay, thanks," Nate said, smoothing down the back of his hair. "Sorry, man," he said to Peyton.

Debra shifted her gaze to me and smiled broadly. "Oh, hey, *Lay*la!" she said with a quick wave of her fingers. "*Love* the outfit."

Bitch!

"Thanks! *Love* the hair," I replied. "Are two-inch roots back in?"

Yes! That forty minutes of comeback brainstorming in Spanish was *good*. Debra narrowed her eyes at me, then disappeared inside the gym. Luckily Nate was too distracted by being thwarted from our kiss to notice the cattiness.

"Can we meet later?" he asked. "After practice?"

"Sure. Actually, I'm supposed to help this new kid catch up in Spanish, so I'll be in the library," I said, trying to ignore the way my pulse raced at the thought of meeting up with Ian.

Pulse racing over two guys at the same time? Not good. Possibly a prelude to a coronary, actually.

"Cool," Nate said. "See you then."

Yes, you will, I thought, watching him go. *And hopefully I'll finally be getting that kiss.*

"Okay, that takes care of next week's assignments," I said, checking my watch. All of the *Reporter* editors were gathered around the long table in the center of the newsroom for our meeting, which was already running long. The last thing I wanted was for Ian to think he was getting dissed on his first day at a new school. I had to wrap this up. "One more order of business—The Kensington Daze."

"Ugh. The dreaded gossip forum," Cara said with a groan, tipping her head back. We had argued for hours about whether or not to start up the forum and Cara had never been a big fan, but I didn't have time to debate it with her again.

"How's it going, Mike?" I asked.

Cara looked at her boyfriend like he was some kind of evil traitor. It wasn't the poor guy's fault that he was in charge of the website. He was just good with computers.

"Uh . . . it's going well," he said, clearing his throat and averting his gaze from Cara. He scratched at his brown crew cut and glanced at his notes. "Actually, it's a hit. It's only been up and running since last Wednesday and it's already doubled our web traffic."

"And thanks to that fact I got two more advertisers this week without even trying," Anna Schultz added.

Cara shook her head. "I don't know. I still don't like it. A no-rules forum like that where anyone can post anything they want can get really ugly. We're supposed to be a serious newspaper. Doesn't encouraging gossip destroy our credibility?"

"Cara, this is *The Reporter*, not *The New York Times*," I said. "You've gotta give the people what they want."

"If you say so," Cara replied.

"Okay, I have to go," I said, gathering my things. "We're all set, right?"

"Good to go," Mike said.

"Great. I'll catch you guys tomorrow."

"Don't do anything I wouldn't do!" Cara called after me as I hustled out of the room.

"Yeah, right."

I glanced over my shoulder at her. She and Mike were already cozying up to one another as he helped her put on her jacket.

Don't do anything Cara wouldn't do? She wouldn't even be meeting with Ian, just in case Mike might get jealous. I'd already gone against her warning.

When I got to the library I made the rounds, checking every table and hidden nook. No sign of Ian. Maybe he had blown *me* off.

But then I saw a flash of orange out of the corner of my eye and paused. Ian was outside on the front lawn of the school, talking on his cell phone. What was he doing out there? Wasn't it, like, freezing out? I dropped my books and headed for the door, but the second I opened it, I regretted my decision. Whomever Ian was talking to, he was clearly not happy.

"You must be joking! That git!?" he shouted. "What the hell do you see in him?" He paced back and forth as he sputtered. "No! Well that's just *fine*! Go away with him on holiday, then! I didn't want you here anyway!"

Oh, God. He was breaking up with his girlfriend. And I was eavesdropping. I started to back into the library again, but at that moment he looked up and saw me. He put up a finger and I stopped.

"In fact, I already met someone as well," he said defiantly.

He waved me toward him. I didn't move a muscle. Was he kidding?

"In fact, she's right here." He waved more urgently. "Her name is Layla."

Tentatively, I stepped out into the cold and edged toward him, wrapping my arms around myself. What did he want me to do?

"Yeah. Maybe I'll take *her* to the Bloodworms concert, right?" he said into the phone. "What do you think about that?"

"The Bloodworms?" I blurted.

Ian's eyes lit up. "Yeah. That was her."

I couldn't believe it. Did Ian really have tickets to the Bloodworms concert? Those had been sold out since exactly seven minutes after they'd gone on sale. Cara and I had lied to our parents and slept out on the street to buy them, only to be turned away after more than eighteen hours of freezing our butts off. I would have *died* to go to that concert.

"She's just *dying* to go with me. Aren't you, love?" he said, his eyes widened hopefully. Nice mind read, dude. "Aren't you?" he repeated pointedly.

He looked seriously desperate. Should I help him save face with this chick? Why not? At least it wasn't like I'd have to fake the enthusiasm.

"Oh, definitely," I said loudly enough to be heard on the other end. "I can't *wait*."

Ian grinned and flashed me a thumbs-up. "Good. Fine, then," he said into the phone. "Good-bye!"

He slapped the phone closed and groaned in frustration.

"Girlfriend?" I said sympathetically.

"Ex-girlfriend now," he clarified. "I'm gone for two measly weeks and she's already moved on to my best mate."

"Ouch."

"Tell me about it," he said. He blew out a sigh. "Thanks for that."

"No problem."

"Well, here." He pulled out his wallet, extracted a ticket from inside the billfold, and handed it over. "I suppose you've earned that."

I stared down at the little white and blue slip. It was, in fact, a ticket to the Bloodworms. A *front row* ticket. This was incredible!

"You have to be kidding me," I said.

"Look, I already have the tickets and so far you're the only person at this bloody school who's been nice to me the whole day, so why not?" he said. "It's not like I have a date anymore anyway. Besides, you obviously fancy them."

I blinked and stared at the ticket. Something about what he had just said made me pause. "A date." Did he mean that *this* would be a date? And if so, could I really do that?

I looked up at Ian and bit my bottom lip. "I don't know. . . ."

"Come on. It's the Bloodworms. Front row," he said. "Are you really gonna turn that down? Am I that hideously unattractive?"

I looked up at his grinning face and my heart thumped extra hard. He knew he was so *not* unattractive. And he was also right. There was no way I could turn down a chance like this. Besides, one concert with another guy didn't necessarily constitute cheating. Even if there was this sort of sizzling, kinetic, almost magnetic attraction thing between us.

"Okay," I said finally. I wondered for a few seconds if I should tell Ian about Nate, but decided that it wasn't important right now. I ignored the unsettling feeling of guilt that sprang up in my stomach. "But only because you're a charity case with no friends and I feel sorry for you."

"Your benevolence overwhelms me," he said with a coy look in his eye.

"Good," I replied, slipping the ticket into my pocket. "Now let's go study."

I was just saying good-bye to Ian in the hallway when Nate came around the corner with his gym bag. His brow knit as he approached and he watched Ian until he was all the way through the lobby and out the front door. I squared my shoulders and took a deep breath. I had already resolved to be upfront with Nate and tell him about the concert. More upfront than I'd been with Ian about having a boyfriend. I was not about lying and sneaking around. But now that he was here, I was feeling sort of nervous about the whole thing. What if he flipped out? What if he blew me off? Or worse, what if he didn't even care?

"Who was that?" Nate asked, pausing in front of me. He was all pink from the shower and his blond hair was slicked back from his face.

"Oh. That was Ian, the new guy," I said casually. "Remember? I told you I was helping him catch up in Spanish."

"*That* was the new guy?" Nate asked. "He looks like he's twenty-five."

"He's not," I said with a laugh.

"Well, it was nice of you to help him," Nate said, adjusting the strap of his bag on his shoulder.

"Thanks. Actually, he gave me something as sort of a thank you," I said tentatively. "A ticket to the Bloodworms concert."

Nate scoffed. Not exactly a reaction I had expected.

"Some thank you."

"What?"

"You *like* that band?" Nate asked, shocked.

"Doesn't everybody?"

"Whatever you say," he replied with a smile. "So who else is going?"

Gulp. Apparently he hadn't gotten the point.

"Just me and him," I said.

The smile instantly died.

"Oh," Nate said.

"Oh . . . what?" I said.

Nate cleared his throat and shrugged. "Oh, nothing. That's cool."

"It is?" I asked.

His ears were turning bright red. "Sure. Why wouldn't it be?"

Um, maybe because you like me? Maybe because we spent the entire weekend together? Maybe because you *so* want to kiss me?

Or maybe he didn't. Maybe he hadn't kissed me yet because he wasn't actually attracted to me. Or maybe he'd finally heard those rumors Debra had been spewing and was minutes from breaking up with me anyway.

Either way, I suddenly felt like a total idiot for even entertaining the idea of feeling guilty. Clearly Nate couldn't have cared less.

Well, fine. If he didn't care, neither did I. I wasn't going to waste my time here.

"So, you want a ride home?" he asked.

"No, thanks," I said, striding by him. "I've made other plans."

The last thing I wanted to do just then was sit alone with him in a car for fifteen minutes, wondering where I stood. As much as I hated the bus, it was looking like a solid alternative.

four

The next day after school I stayed late at the *Reporter* office, polishing up my latest article for the paper. Almost everyone had finished up their work already and headed home, so I had the place to myself. Of course, the second I started trying to concentrate, my thoughts turned to Nate. We had barely said hello to each other today. I was still mad about his total lack of reaction to my maybe-date with Ian. And apparently, he was mad at me, too, though I had no idea what I'd actually done.

So what? a little voice in my mind asked. *There are other guys out there. And besides, he doesn't like the Bloodworms. Can you really be serious about a guy like that?*

I smirked at my sarcastic inner voice—always there

when I needed her. That was it. No more dwelling. Not when there was work to do. I reached into my bag for my iPod and found a note attached to it.

You suck! Love, Cara.

She must have stuck it in there earlier in the day. She wasn't too happy about my going to the concert without her. I smiled, crossed out her note and wrote:

Be nice or I won't get you a T-shirt! Love, Layla.

Then I stuck the note into the pocket of the green hoodie she'd left hanging on the back of her chair.

I hooked up my iPod to my computer and let the Bloodworms rip through the speakers as I got to work. Once I was engrossed, the work went pretty quickly. When I was done I decided to check out the online edition of the paper to see how many hits we were getting.

I clicked open the "editors only" page and typed in my password. Instantly that day's numbers popped up.

Whoa. Two thousand and thirty four hits in one day? That was amazing! Mike wasn't kidding. The Kensington Daze was reeling in the readers. Sorry, Cara. Looks like I had been right about the Daze all along.

I clicked on an icon shaped like a chatting head and was instantly connected to the forum. There was a subsection for nearly every kind of gossip you might be interested in: teachers, wacky sightings around the school, cafeteria food, worst outfits of the day, and, of course, who was hooking up with whom.

After reading about some of today's wacky sightings, I went right to the "Hookups and Breakups" board. That's where the juicy gossip really got flowing. A girl had to have her guilty pleasures. I read the first posting.

"Truth hurts" writes:

Layla Carter and Nate Henry: Anyone else shocked at this pairing?

I took a deep breath. It wasn't like I was surprised at the comment. I had known from day one that people would be shocked to see the two of us together. I steeled myself and kept reading.

HOW has it lasted this long??? Does the poor guy not know that his new girlfriend has been with every guy in the school?

Oh, God. This was very *not* good. Debra. It had to be. What, exactly, did that evil witch have against me? I was about to type back a "bite me" reply when my eyes fell on the message.

"Share the love" responds:

Maybe he just wants a piece for himself. Why should he be the only guy at Kensington not getting Layla'd?

What? This could not be happening. Who did these people think they were? I liked to date around, but who doesn't?

"Layla'd and loved it" writes:

I was Layla'd once. In a blue convertible. It was goooood!!

A blue convertible? Huh? I'd never been in a blue convertible in my life.

"Reality Check" writes:

Get over yourself. Every guy at Kensington has been

Layla'd. I don't think they let you graduate unless you've had a taste.

I was starting to feel sick. Sick and humiliated and skeeved. I was about to shut the computer down, my self-preservation instinct kicking in, when one of the postings stopped me dead in my tracks.

"Purity" *writes:*

Nate Henry deserves so much better! If you're reading this, Nate, take my advice. Dump the girl while you still have your dignity.

Nate. Oh, God, Nate. Had he read this? Did he believe it? Was that why he hadn't cared that I was going out with Ian?

I had to call him. I had to explain. I fumbled for my bag and pulled out my cell phone, but paused before dialing his number.

No. Hold up. Wait a second. I was not going to be that girl. There was nothing wrong with the fact that I had dated a lot of guys and I was not going to be ashamed of who I was. Plus, everything on this stupid message board was a lie. If Nate wanted to believe them without even asking me, that was his problem. His loss.

I got up, turned off the computer, and slipped my phone back into my bag. The gossip-mongers of The Kensington Daze could kiss my ass.

Ten minutes later I had ducked under a Plexiglas bus shelter, cowering away from the pouring rain. As if it hadn't been enough to have hundreds of my fictitious exploits shoved down my throat, now the weather had turned against me, too. Could nothing go right in my life?

Suddenly I heard the roar of a motorcycle engine. I looked up the street and saw a single headlight hurtling through the rain—headed straight toward me.

My heart stopped beating. I looked left and right and realized I had nowhere to go. I was literally boxed in and the psycho was still coming! This was it. This was the end of my life.

I was too scared to move. I closed my eyes and screamed at the top of my lungs. I heard a screech of tires, a deafening roar, and I was suddenly splashed from head to toe with ice-cold rain water. I took a deep, shaky breath.

Okay, I'm alive. I'm alive. I'm wet, but I'm alive.

Carefully, I opened one eye. The motorcycle's front wheel was mere inches from my leg.

"What the hell is the matter with you?!" I shouted.

As I struggled for breath, the rider whipped off his black helmet and shook his hair out.

"Are you all right?"

Holy goddess of the earth. I was staring right into the concerned hazel eyes of Drew Sullivan. *The* Drew Sullivan. The literal man of my dreams. I had just screamed at *Drew Sullivan.*

"I . . . I . . ."

Drew stepped closer to me, studying my face, which gave me ample time to scope him out. He looked just the same as I remembered him: about six-foot-three, longish brown hair, battered leather motorcycle jacket over faded jeans. He looked as dangerous as ever.

Dangerous and sexy.

"Are you in shock?" he asked me.

"Yeah," I said. Then I laughed. "I mean, no. No. I'm fine."

"The rain sometimes screws with my brakes," he said, gesturing over his shoulder. "Guess I should have that fixed."

"Yeah. Maybe," I said.

"Well, sorry. If you're okay . . ." he said, turning to go.

No. Don't go. Say something, Layla! Anything!

"Still got the old Norton, huh?" I blurted.

Ugh! I may as well have had STALKER printed across my forehead.

Drew looked at me, narrowing his gorgeous eyes. "Do I know you?"

For a moment all I could do was stare back. I definitely couldn't say, "You were my god two years ago," or, "I memorized the Norton owner's manual two years ago so that I could impress you just in case you ever decided to talk to me."

"I . . . I've seen you around," I said after a moment. "It's not every day you spot a red Norton."

"You know bikes." It was a statement, not a question. And he seemed impressed. Sort of.

"I'm Layla," I said finally.

"Drew," he replied with a nod.

Well. Definitely not a talker, this one. But no matter. I had always regretted the fact that I never got up the guts to talk to him back when he was at Kensington and now I'd been handed a second chance. There was no way I was going to let an opportunity like this pass me by.

"Actually, you could do me a little favor," I said. "Since you almost killed me and all."

Drew looked wary. "What kind of favor?"

"The bus is taking *forever*," I said, looking down the street, just hoping the 210 wasn't coming around the corner right then. "And it's only really drizzling now so maybe your brakes are okay . . ." I said, looking up at the sky.

Drew looked up, too. Then he sort of blew a sigh through his nose.

"Want a ride?"

I grinned and tried very hard not to jump up and down. "Definitely."

Drew nodded. "Get on." He straddled his bike, grabbed his extra helmet, and held it out. I was giddy as I climbed on behind him and tentatively wrapped my arms around him. Around Drew Sullivan.

I think I drooled a little bit.

"Where to?" he asked.

"Two-twenty-two Robin's Way," I said.

He nodded and we were off, flying down the street. My heart pounded in my ears as I gasped for breath. This had to be the single most exhilarating moment of my life. Closing my eyes, I tried to memorize this feeling of wind, rain, leather, and the warmth of his body. Stray raindrops spattered against my visor, and I rested my head against his back as I held on tightly.

Me and Drew Sullivan on a thrill ride through town. Who would have ever thought it was possible? I wished everyone in school could see me just then.

Way too soon he slowed the bike to a stop in front of my house.

"Huh," he said, studying my house as he lifted off his helmet.

I looked up the long drive at my mother's pottery studio, which was attached to our house. My mother did her work in the studio and sold it in the little shop space up front. I tried to see what he saw. What had made him go, "huh."

"What?" I asked, lifting my leg over the back of the bike.

"You live here?" he said, nodding toward my house. "With that pottery woman?"

I laughed uncertainly. Did he have a problem with my mother? "That pottery woman is my mom."

Drew frowned thoughtfully. "Cool."

Then it hit me in a rush. Drew was an artist—a painter. Another thing he was known for, outside his hotness, was all the artwork Mrs. Haley had entered in those competitions back when he was still in school. Maybe he was actually *impressed* that my mom was the pottery woman.

"Do you want to come check out the studio?" I asked, quickly running over Mom's schedule in my head. Safe! Mom taught an advanced pottery class at the community college on Tuesday afternoons. She wouldn't be around to do anything embarrassing in front of him, like call me "sweet cheeks."

"Cool," he said.

We walked together toward the studio. I could hear my heart banging against my rib cage plain as day. Drew Sullivan in my house. Me and Drew Sullivan, alone, in my house. Well, at least in the studio, which was close enough.

Maybe fantasies really did come true!

I fumbled for my keys and opened the door to the shop. A dozen tiny little door chimes tinkled. Drew looked up and stared at them as if he'd never seen something like that before.

"Well, this is it!" I said, locking the door behind us. Couldn't have any of my mother's customers walking in and spoiling the moment.

Drew walked slowly along the shelves of pottery, studying some of the more abstract pieces.

"I've always wanted to learn how to do this," he said sincerely.

I swallowed hard. "I could . . . uh . . . teach you."

It was amazing how nervous he made me. No guys made me this nervous. But then again, this *was* Drew Sullivan.

"Really? That'd be cool." His eyes lit right up and for a split second he looked like a little kid hyped up on too much sugar. But then, he relaxed again. "I mean, if you've got the time. Whatever," he said, all cool.

"I'm not doing anything now," I announced.

Nice. Way to be lame.

"Why don't you get an apron?" I said, pointing at the hooks on the wall. "I'll get the clay ready."

"Cool," Drew said with a bobbing nod.

I turned and pulled some fresh clay out of the bucket. My hands were trembling. I took a deep breath and tried to calm my nerves. If he saw how freaked out I was he was going to think I was a total tool.

"Ready?" I said.

Drew had a gray apron tied loosely around his waist. He held out a red one for me.

My hands full of clay, I stepped toward him, into a shaft of struggling sunlight creeping through the overhead sky-light.

"Could you . . . ?"

"Sure."

He stepped closer to me and slipped the loop of the apron over my head. My heart was beating so loud that he had to be able to hear it. I looked up into his eyes and he stared down into mine.

Then, ever so slowly, he reached behind me and lifted my long hair over the apron loop. It tumbled down my back and my breath turned shallow.

"You have amazing eyes," Drew said. "They change color every time I look at them."

Every inch of my skin throbbed.

"Yours are pretty amazing, too," I said.

He stepped so close to me our knees touched. His gaze

never left mine.

He's going to kiss me, I thought. *Drew Sullivan is going to kiss me!*

And then, he cupped my face with his hands, pulled me to him, and made my fantasy come true.

five

I dropped the wad of clay I was holding to the ground and closed my eyes. Kissing Drew Sullivan was everything I had imagined it would be, only better. His hands were rough and calloused, but gentle against my face. His body was warm and smelled faintly of gasoline and rain. As I wrapped my arms around him, he pulled me tightly to his chest as if I couldn't be close enough.

Drew backed me toward the wall and I went willingly, wanting more than anything to feel him pressed up against me. But then my butt slammed into my mother's work table. Something crashed to the floor and Drew instantly pulled away.

"Oh, God. Sorry," he said.

I struggled for breath, as confused as if I'd just been

jolted out of a deep sleep. Drew was looking at the ground. One of my mother's signature bowls lay in shards on the concrete floor.

"Oh. It's okay," I said. "Don't worry about it."

I was dying for him to kiss me again, but he was slowly backing away, ripping the apron off over his head.

"I better go," he said.

"You don't have to—"

"No. I really do," he replied, gunning for the door.

My insides drooped. He couldn't get away from me fast enough. "Okay. Well then, I guess I—"

But I never got to finish my sentence. The bells tinkled and Drew was out the door. I opened the window blinds so I could watch him go. He speed-walked to his bike and peeled out, racing down the street so fast you'd think the house was about to blow up.

Okay. What the hell had just happened here? *He* had kissed *me*, hadn't he? And was it just me or was that one of the most amazing kisses of all time? Why had he run like that?

I took a deep breath and tried to wrap my brain around everything. Drew Sullivan. I had just been kissed by Drew Sullivan. I touched my still throbbing lips with my fingertips. If someone had told me this morning that *that* was going to happen today, I would have laughed my ass off.

The question was, would it ever happen again? God, I hoped so. If only I could figure out what had made him bolt.

I was about to turn away from the window when I saw Nate's silver Prius pull into my driveway.

Oh, my God. Nate. What was *he* doing here?

Okay, one guy crisis at a time, Layla.

I shook my hair back, cleared my throat, and opened the shop door. Nate was just getting out of his car and he looked up at me, startled.

"Hey," he said.

"Hey," I replied flatly.

"Was that Drew Sullivan I just saw pulling out of here?" he asked as he closed his car door.

Snagged!

Wait a minute. I wasn't even sure Nate wanted to date me anymore. It wasn't like he'd talked to me once the entire day. So technically I hadn't done anything wrong with Drew.

"Yeah. He came by to check out my mom's work," I said. "So what's up?"

Nate looked at me quizzically as he approached. "Why are you being so weird?"

"I'm not being weird," I said, leading him into the shop and closing the door behind us. "I'm just wondering what you're doing here."

"What? I can't drop by to see my girlfriend?" Nate asked.

Wha-huh? "I'm sorry. Did I just hallucinate? I thought I heard you call me your girlfriend."

"You're angry," he said, pocketing his keys.

"No. Not angry. Just wondering how you can call

someone your girlfriend after not talking to her all day," I said.

And, hello! You haven't even kissed me yet! I just kissed Drew Sullivan who I never talked to before today and you haven't kissed me yet!

Right. That might not be the best point to make just now.

"I'm sorry about today," Nate said. "But I was a little mad at you, too. I mean, you stood there and basically told me you were going out on a date with another guy like it was no big deal."

"Well, you reacted like it was no big deal," I pointed out.

"What was I supposed to do? Beg you not to go out with him?" he asked. "A guy has to have *some* pride," he added with a grin.

"Oh," I said, looking at my feet. "So you're saying you *were* upset?"

"Of course I was," he said. "You're my girl."

Nate reached out and wrapped his arms around my waist. A sharp stab of guilt hit me right through the heart. If only he knew that five minutes ago I'd been groping another guy about ten feet from where he was standing. I doubt if he'd be calling me his "girl" then.

"It's not a date," I heard myself say, trying to assuage *some* of my guilt. "We're really just going as friends."

"Well, that's good to hear," Nate said. "Because I like you, Layla. A lot. And I'm sort of hoping you like me, too."

47

I looked into his eyes and smiled. It was amazing what could change in twenty-four hours.

"I do," I told him honestly.

"Good," he said. "So I was thinking, since we like each other so much and all—"

I laughed.

"Maybe you'd want to go to the Valentine's Day dance with me this weekend?" he asked.

I blinked. Even with all the guys I had dated I had never actually gone to a school dance before. Not once. Probably because the kinds of guys I usually dated didn't *do* school dances.

"I know it's cheesy, but Friday's gonna be our one-month anniversary and Saturday is Valentine's Day, and I just thought—"

"It's not cheesy," I said, my heart full.

I couldn't believe how sweet he was, thinking about V-Day and anniversaries. He really liked me. Really cared about me. And I had almost screwed it all up. For what? A ticket to a concert? A kiss with a guy who had bolted out of here like I was some freakshow? If Nate had shown up here any earlier he would have caught me in a love clench with Drew Sullivan and I never would have had the chance to hear all this.

"So, what do you say?" Nate asked.

"I'm in," I said. "As long as I don't have to wear some fluffy red ball gown or something." Actually, what was I going to wear? Mental note: go shopping with Cara.

Nate smiled. "You can wear whatever you want. You

can wear jeans for all I care. In fact, I've always thought jeans were a good look for you."

"Really?" I said, giddy.

"Really."

He looked deep into my eyes and his expression grew serious. For the second time this afternoon I knew for sure I was about to be kissed, and my heart turned over in my chest.

Just let it be good, I thought. *Let it be even better than it was with Drew.*

Nate reached out, tucked my hair behind my ear, then leaned in. Just before our lips met, my breath caught in my chest. He pulled me gently to him and my eyes fluttered closed.

It was a sweet kiss. A tender kiss. Totally the opposite of Drew's rough, sexy, searching kiss.

And just as perfect, in a totally different way.

When Nate finally pulled away, I felt tears prickling at the corners of my eyes. This had to be the single most baffling day of my life.

"I've been wanting to do that for a long time," Nate said.

I reached out and hugged him, hard, resting my chin on his shoulder so he wouldn't see the total confusion in my eyes. "Me, too," I said.

Now if only I could figure out what to do next.

"I'm evil, Cara. I am totally, totally evil."

I paced back and forth in front of my bedroom window

while Cara stared at me from the foot of my bed. She'd barely spoken since I'd started relating the tale of my afternoon of debauchery.

"You're not evil. In fact, I'd say you're just *really* lucky," she said.

"You are not listening to a word I'm saying!" I told her. "I kissed Drew Sullivan and then five minutes later, I kissed Nate. I've been going out with Nate for three weeks and I kissed Drew Sullivan *first*! What the heck does that tell you?"

"Uh, that Nate could learn a thing or two from Drew about taking the initiative?" Cara said, raising her eyebrows.

"You are not helping!" I said, throwing up my hands.

"Actually, I think I am. You did not kiss these guys. They kissed you. You are not at fault here," Cara told me, grabbing a nail file from my desk and sitting back down again.

"Semantics," I said.

"Hey. You're the future lawyer," Cara told me, gesturing with the file. "You tell me. Could you get a client off on that argument?"

"Can we focus here, Cara? What am I going to do?" I asked her.

"Okay. Here's the real question," she said. She lifted her leg onto the bed and turned to me, her eyes sparkling with curiosity. "Which one was better?"

I groaned, remembering the feeling of Drew's hands on my skin, then the gentle touch of Nate's lips. "That's just it.

They were both equally good. Just in different ways. But they both gave me, like, the tinglies, you know?" I said, giving a little shiver.

Cara narrowed her eyes at me. "You know, I think I've been wrong all this time. You should totally keep dating around."

"*What?*" That had to be the most shocking thing I'd heard all day.

"That way I can keep living vicariously through you," she said.

"Ha-ha."

"Hey. Mike's been kissing me so long it's been a *while* since I got the tinglies," Cara said.

"See, now that's just sad," I told her.

"Tell me about it." She got up and dropped the nail file back on my desk. "Sorry, babe. I gotta go. If I'm late for dinner my mom will send out the dogs." She slapped me on the shoulder with confidence. "Don't worry. I'm *sure* you'll figure out which mega-hot guy to choose. If only we all had such problems."

"Thanks for your help," I said facetiously, dropping down onto my bed.

"Anytime," she said with a laugh.

"Layla, can you pass me the red pepper?" my mom asked, reaching behind her as she stirred our dinner at the stove.

I shook myself out of my Nate-and-Drew induced stupor and grabbed the spice for her.

51

"Thanks, sweet cheeks," she said, winking as I handed her the bottle.

I sighed hugely. "*Why* do you have to call me that?"

"Because when you were born your father said you had the sweetest little cheeks he'd ever seen and I had to agree," my mother said, leaning over to kiss one of said cheeks.

"Right. So glad that stuck even though he didn't," I said, dropping down onto one of the stools by the kitchen counter.

My mother glanced at me over her shoulder, then brushed her hands off on her apron, lowered the heat on our tofu and black bean chili, and turned around.

"Okay, kid. What's eating you?" she asked, swinging her long braid over her shoulder.

"Nothing," I said, slouching back against the counter. "It's just, do you ever think marrying Dad was just one colossal mistake?"

"Never," my mother said without missing a beat.

"Not even after all the crap hit the fan?" I asked.

"We loved each other, and I'll always trust that," she replied. "But people change, and sometimes you just can't live with each other anymore." She turned and stirred the pot a few times. "Why are you bringing this up now?"

"I've just been thinking about the whole love thing," I said. "Wondering whether we really are supposed to be with only *one* person."

Mom tossed a dash of chili pepper into the pot and turned to me again.

"Honey, did something happen with Nate?"

"Not exactly," I answered, squirming. "I was just wondering how you know who's right for you. There are so many interesting people out there . . . how do you choose just one?"

"It's just something you know," she said. "I can't explain it. Like I knew with your father."

"But he *wasn't* the one," I pointed out. "Not in the end."

A grim expression came over my mother's face. One that was completely unnatural for her. "He was the one for me, but it seems I wasn't the one for him," she said. "Your father, he . . . needed his freedom."

Yeah, so he could go off and live with that new girlfriend of his. I looked at the floor, feeling suddenly awful for bringing this up. How selfish was I, dredging up bad memories for my mom just so I could try to figure out what I was doing with Nate and Drew? Chances were, I'd never even see Drew again, so this would all be a moot point anyway.

I was with Nate. And I was staying with Nate. Case closed.

"Sorry, Mom," I said, hopping off the stool and giving her a kiss. "Let's talk about something else."

I opened the cabinet for some bowls and bumped it closed with my hip.

"Good idea," she said, clearing her throat. "So, how's the school paper?"

She went back to cooking and we were officially off on a much safer tangent.

As I set the table I felt more confident and sure of

myself than I had all afternoon. Nate was a good guy, a nice guy, and he cared about me. I wasn't going to hurt him the way my dad had hurt my mom.

At least, not if I could help it.

six

I rounded the corner on my way to my locker on Wednesday morning and stopped in my tracks. Ian was leaning against the locker next to mine, one foot up on the wall behind him, wearing a brown suede jacket and looking beyond hot. He held two cups of coffee in his hands and sipped from one.

Great. Bachelor number three. Just what I needed.

Okay. I had to nip this thing in the bud. I was going to the Valentine's Day dance with Nate. I wanted to be with Nate. Monogamy was the way to go.

I took a deep breath and approached my locker. Ian smiled when he saw me and stood up straight.

"Morning, lovely."

His voice sent pleasant reverberations throughout

my body. God, monogamy sucked.

"For you."

He held out one of the coffee cups and it smelled unbelievable, but I had to go against my every instinct and give him the cold shoulder. I just had to.

"I'm not big into caffeine," I said, starting on my combination.

"Come on. All you Americans are addicted to coffee. It's what you're all about," he said.

"Well, not this American," I lied.

I reached into my locker and pulled out my textbooks for the first few classes of the day. Why didn't he just leave already? Why did he have to keep looking me up and down with those sexy dark eyes of his?

"So, I was hoping we could meet again today," he said. "Still have a bit of catching up to do for class."

"I can't today," I said flatly.

"Oh, come on, Lay-la-la," he said teasingly, leaning his shoulder into the locker and nudging me with his other arm. "You promised your teacher you'd help me. You wouldn't want me to report you now, would you?"

I glanced over at him and smiled. I couldn't help it. One cannot look at a face that gorgeous and not blush and smile.

"Fine," I said, caving. "But this is the last time. I have a feeling you're faking all this Spanish ignorance of yours."

Damn. That sounded more flirtatious than I realized. But I guess that was just me—just the way I talked when cute guys were involved. What was I supposed to do, completely overhaul my personality?

Ian's grin widened. "Now *why* would I do that?" he asked.

I rolled my eyes at him and slammed my locker door, smiling even though I wanted to kick myself.

As much as my conscience fought it, I couldn't seem to stop myself from hanging out with him.

"Whatever. Just be in the library after the bell," I said. "Don't be late."

"Yes, ma'am," he said with a smirk. "Wouldn't want to be punished or anything."

There were about ten million flirty comebacks for that one jumping around in my brain and Ian was just standing there waiting for one.

Can't do it. Don't do it! I scolded myself.

It took all my effort not to toss some witty remark back at him.

"Ugh!" I finally threw my hands up, turned, and walked away as fast as my high-heeled boots allowed.

These guys were not making this easier on me. Not one bit.

That afternoon I walked into my room, slammed the door, and flopped down on my bed. There was something wrong with me. There truly was. I had just spent the entire afternoon flirting with Ian like there was no tomorrow. Once he got me alone there was nothing I could do to resist it, and once I got started there was no stopping me.

I was insane. I could not control myself.

I scrounged in my bag for my iPod and hooked myself up, tuning into the latest Bloodworms downloads. Then I laid back and closed my eyes again. I had to get a grip. I had to figure out what I was going to do. If I was going to stick with Nate, I had to stick with only Nate. He was not the kind of guy who you casually dated.

But hanging out with Ian was so much fun. And all day my thoughts had kept returning to Drew's kiss. Drew's hands. Drew's body pressed against mine.

Argh!

I turned up the volume and took a deep breath. Suddenly I saw myself with Ian at the Bloodworms concert. We were throwing ourselves around the mosh pit like total lunatics, having the time of our lives. Then we were lifted up for a crowd surf, being passed along from hand to hand, laughing the whole time. Ian reached out and grabbed for my hand and that telltale sizzle of attraction rushed through me. What would it be like if we kissed? If just looking at him made my body heat skyrocket, would kissing him cause spontaneous combustion? And if so, what was I waiting for?

The song ended and one of the Bloodworms's slow love ballads filled my ears. Suddenly I was in Nate's arms, dancing in the center of the Kensington High gym at the Valentine's Day ball. He looked gorgeous in a black and white tuxedo, his eyes focused only on me. My heart pounded as Nate held me close and we swayed back and forth under twinkling white lights. I felt totally safe in his arms. Safe and warm and loved.

"I love you, Layla," he said quietly.

Laying there on my bed, I smiled.

Then, just as Nate leaned in to kiss me, the song changed again to one of the Bloodworms's rare instrumentals. Suddenly I was back in my mom's studio, and Drew was the one kissing me.

But this time when we backed up together, we missed the table and he pressed me up against the cool wall. His lips parted mine, and I felt his hands running through my hair. Then he broke away from my mouth and began kissing my neck. He moved toward my ear and his breath warmed me, sending goose bumps all down my side. In a husky voice he whispered, "I've always wanted to be with you, Layla. Always."

Just then the song ended. I sat up straight, my heart pounding.

Thank you, imagination!

Why did I have to settle for one guy? I mean, if only one of them made me feel this way, then fine. I would be okay with monogamy. But that wasn't the case. All three of these guys made my head spin. And I couldn't choose. I just couldn't. If I gave up on even one of them I would always wonder what could have been.

I was only seventeen. The convent would have to wait.

"That's it. This is just stupid," I said aloud. I would go to the dance with Nate and to the concert with Ian. And if Drew happened to show up again, I would just see where things went. This was my life. I could live it however I wanted.

I grabbed my cell phone out of my bag and scrolled to the calendar to make it official.

First I typed: *Nate, Dance, Saturday, February 14.*

Then I pulled the ticket Ian gave me from my wallet and checked out the date. Without thinking I started to enter it into the calendar.

Ian, Concert . . . February 14.

Oh, crap.

Apparently I had a bigger problem than I'd realized.

seven

Thursday morning I stood at the front door of my house, waiting for Cara and yawning nonstop. I had barely slept at all, trying to figure out what I was going to do. The Valentine's Day dance with Nate would be amazing, but front row tickets to the Bloodworms was a once in a lifetime chance. After hours of tossing and turning I still hadn't decided what to do, and now I had to go to school and face them both.

Who was I going to ditch? And how was I going to tell him? Ian would probably take it better than Nate, but then he'd have no one to go to the concert with. But if I blew off Nate, he'd definitely break up with me. And I wasn't ready to lose him just yet. And to top it all off, part of me just wished Drew would show up on his bike and take me away from all of it.

I was totally screwed.

Suddenly, my cell phone rang. Saved from my own thoughts.

"Hey, Cara. Where are you?" I said into the phone.

"Layla, I am *so* sorry. My car died," Cara said.

"Oh, no. Are you okay?" I said.

"Yeah. Just frustrated. My dad and I are at the mechanic right now trying to figure out what's wrong. Can you get another ride?"

"Sure. Don't worry about it," I said, even though my mother had already left to run errands. Cara sounded stressed out enough without me making her feel guilty. "I'll see you later."

We hung up and I grabbed my warmer coat from the coat rack. I guess I was going to be hoofing it to the bus stop. What a way to start the day.

I was about halfway down the block, already seriously regretting not having changed my footwear also, when I heard the familiar sound of a motorcycle engine roaring toward me. My heart caught in my throat and I paused just as Drew Sullivan pulled up alongside me and pulled his helmet off.

What had I said about Drew showing up? Just see what happened? Looked like we were about to find out.

"Hey," he said.

"Hey."

Play it cool. Just, play it cool.

"Where you headed?" he asked.

"Oh, school," I said, feeling like a kindergartener.

He nodded and looked off down the street. Then he looked back at me. "Feel like ditching?"

Wow. Talk about out of left field. Ditching school? With Drew Sullivan? Could anything be more tempting?

"What did you have in mind?" I heard myself ask.

"Well, I gotta go to my buddy's garage and get a part for my bike, but after that I'm free," he said. "We could do whatever."

Ditching school. That was so not me. I may have dated a few dangerous guys in my time, but I had never done anything all that dangerous myself. Still, this was Drew Sullivan. Asking me to hang out with him all day. Plus there was the added benefit of not having to go to school and deal with Nate and Ian. But just watch this show up on the Kensington Daze.

"Okay," I said finally. "Sounds cool."

Drew lifted the extra helmet and handed it to me and within seconds, we were off. Seemed like Cara's car breaking down was the best thing that could have happened to me today.

Sigh.

What could possibly be better than riding into the country on the back of Drew Sullivan's motorcycle on one of those randomly almost-balmy February mornings with the sun shining and the wind in your hair? If not for the occasional crippling stab of guilt over skipping school and once again being with a guy who wasn't Nate, it might have been one of the more perfect moments of my life.

"Almost there," Drew called back to me, shouting over the wind and the roar of the bike.

Then, suddenly, the bike lurched and took my stomach right along with it. The engine made a sad, whining sound and Drew cursed under his breath.

"What is it? What's wrong?" I shouted.

He pulled the bike off the road and we bucked to a stop. Drew popped the kickstand down.

"It crapped out," he said, glancing over his shoulder at me. "We're gonna need to walk it."

"How far?" I asked, sliding off the bike.

Drew swung his leg over and pulled his helmet off, shaking his hair out. Damn, I loved it when he did that.

"'Bout a mile," he said.

I looked down at my heeled boots. This was not gonna be pretty. "Unless you want to call your friend," I said, fishing out my cell phone. "Maybe he could tow it or whatever?"

"He never answers during the day," Drew said, kicking the stand up again and grasping the handlebars. "Can't hear over the machines."

Right. I gazed down the road at the nothingness before me and winced. So much for that perfection. But what was I going to do? It was an even farther walk back to town.

"All righty then. Let's go," I said.

"Sorry about this," Drew said.

"It's fine, really."

He started to push his bike and I walked along beside

him. At least he had to take it slow thanks to the heavy load. Speed-walking would have been even worse. Of course now, without the roar of the engine, there was nothing but silence. Awkward, conspicuous silence.

And I couldn't take it.

"So, I never got to thank you for the ride the other day," I said. "You took off kind of fast."

Drew grimaced, staring straight ahead. "Yeah. Sorry about that."

More silence. My heart pounded nervously in my chest. Something told me I should just shut up, but it wasn't my style. I needed to know what he was thinking.

"Where did you run off to?" I asked.

"Nowhere," he said.

"Then why did you—"

"It's just, I never do stuff like that," Drew blurted, glancing at me out of the corner of his eye. "Kiss strange girls."

"Oh, so now I'm strange?" I joked.

"Not *strange*. A stranger. Someone I barely know." He seemed to be struggling for words. "I don't generally do that."

"Oh." I was confused. "So, does that mean you regret it?"

"No. That's the thing." Drew stopped and looked at me over the bike. "I thought I would regret it, but I didn't. I mean, I don't."

My heart fluttered pleasantly as I looked into those hazel eyes I had been daydreaming about for years.

"No?"

Drew smiled ever so slightly. "Not at all."

After that it wouldn't have mattered if I was wearing twenty-inch platforms. I was feeling no pain.

Two hours later I was sitting on a bench in Drew's friend's garage, staring at a year-old copy of *Motorcycle Trend*, bored out of my mind. Watching Drew and his almost-as-hot buddy Lucas work on his bike had been entertaining for the first half hour, but my interest had long since waned.

Except when Drew bent over right in front of me to check something in the engine. That got me every time.

"I can't believe you want to drive this hunk of crap cross country," Lucas said, whipping out a wrench. "You're not gonna even make it to Jersey if we don't completely overhaul this sucker."

"You're driving cross country?" I said. "That's awesome."

"I want to," Drew said, standing up and wiping his hands on his jeans. "Seems like something an artist should do at least once."

Damn. Could he *be* any cooler?

"I gotta go get a part from the back," Lucas said, tossing one of his tools on the concrete floor with a clang. "Sit tight."

"So, almost done?" I asked, my leg bouncing up and down, raring to go.

Drew blew out a sigh. "No, actually. It's gonna be a few more hours."

My heart sunk. A few hours? God help me, but I would have so rather been in history class just then.

"Sorry, Layla," he said. "Lemme call you a cab to take you home. I think there's a company around here."

"A cab? I was hoping we were gonna spend the day together," I said.

Drew looked around at the dingy shop with its peeling paint and its posters of half-naked women posing on hot rods. "Well, if you wanna stay here . . ."

Ten minutes later, I was sitting in the backseat of a Mr. Taxi cab, looking up at him through the open door. Yeah, he was Drew Sullivan, but one could only listen to the wail of a power wrench for so long without going completely insane.

"So," I said.

I was hoping for another kiss. I'll admit it. He'd already as much as told me he was hoping for one, too.

"So," he said. "Sorry. Again."

"No problem. I had fun."

He grinned. "Lies."

"You're right. It sucked. Every minute of it," I teased.

"Dude! Get your ass back in here! I need your help!" Lucas shouted from the open garage door.

"Better go," Drew said.

"Me, too," I replied.

Then he leaned in and my heart skipped around in my chest. I closed my eyes and tilted my head up and—

He kissed me on the forehead.

Huh?

"See ya."

Then the door slammed, the driver hit the gas, and I was on my way back to Kensington, surprised, disappointed, and more confused than ever.

eight

Unfortunately, I had to go back to school. Mom would be home by now and if she found out I'd skipped class, she would ground my butt before you could say "serenity now." As the cab pulled up in front of Kensington High, most of the seniors were pouring out the front door toward me. It was lunchtime and seniors were allowed to leave campus during lunch. Which meant that, most likely, both Ian and Nate would be coming out those doors any second now.

Great. Just what I needed.

I headed for the side door of the school. If I timed it just right I could sneak into the back of the cafeteria before either of them saw me and thereby buy myself a little more time to figure out what I was going to do. I grabbed the door handle and pulled. It was locked.

"Hey, Lay-la-la!"

Mental note: Never apply for a job at the CIA. I turned slowly and looked into those deep, dark eyes. Ian was grinning like the Cheshire Cat. Except he was far more attractive. And less pink.

"You are *so* going to love me," he said.

Exactly what I needed.

"Why's that?" I asked, glancing over his shoulder. I saw Nate and my heart hit the bricks. But he was chatting with some of his basketball buddies on their way to one of their cars and he never looked up.

Thank the Lord. Nate may have been okay with me going to the concert with Ian as friends, but if he found out the date of said concert and that I was even entertaining the idea of going at all, there would definitely be a meltdown.

"Because I scored an invite to the after-concert party at the penthouse."

"The penthouse?" I asked.

"Necro's penthouse apartment in *N . . . Y . . . C*," he said, executing a sexy little dance move to accentuate his point.

My jaw dropped—seriously—straight to the ground.

"Necro? As in Necro Phillips? As in the Bloodworms's lead singer?" I asked, flabbergasted.

"Do you know of any other?"

"*How* the *hell* did you do *that*?" I demanded giddily.

"Join me for lunch and I'll tell you all about it."

He dangled his car keys in front of me. I glanced at the parking lot where a red Jeep Cherokee full of basketball players was just peeling out onto the street.

"Okay," I said with a smile. "You're on."

Ten minutes later, Ian and I were seated across from one another at Pizza Pizza with a small plain pie between us. For the moment, the food was being completely ignored.

"Your dad is with the band," I repeated back to him. "Your dad *works* for the Bloodworms."

Ian shrugged casually. "It's not something I generally noise around, but yeah. He's like their handler when they're on tour. That's why we're here in the States—for the American leg of the worldwide tour."

"Unbelievable. This is just totally unbelievable."

I was going to be hanging out with the Bloodworms. Me. In Necro Phillips's apartment hanging out with the greatest band of all time.

That was, if I blew off Nate and our anniversary/V-Day date.

"Well, believe it, baby," he said, lifting a steaming hot slice out of the pie.

"So, wait a minute, does that mean you'll be leaving school soon?" I asked.

He shook his head. "No. I'm staying in Kensington with my aunt for the rest of the school year so I can graduate. I'll miss the West Coast and Asia, but they're going out again next year, so I can catch it then if I want. Dad said they can always use roadies, and he'll hook me up with the job. I know a bloke who's teaching me to work their sound system, too, so maybe I can do that after I'm graduated."

"Unbelievable," I repeated.

"You said that already," he said with a smirk.

I whacked his arm and picked up my soda. "So, do you like traveling with the band?" I asked.

He took a bite of his pizza and looked at me, surprised. "You're the first person to ever ask me that," he said thoughtfully. "You know, everyone simply assumes it must be fab. But it isn't always so wonderful."

"Why not?" I asked, grabbing a slice for myself. "Aren't they cool?"

"They are, but it's not really much of a home life, is it?" he replied. "My mum does musical theater in England, so she travels most of the time, too, and I'm always popping back and forth between my parents. Plus, I rather wished I could go to one school and stay there. You know . . . have regular friends that I saw from year to year. Some years I didn't go to school at all but had a tutor who traveled with us."

"Sounds good to me," I joked.

He smiled. "You must think I'm a total git. 'Oh, my life is so horrible! I get to hang out with rock stars!'" he fake-whined.

"No, I get it," I assured him. "It sounds like it could be really lonely."

"It can be," he said. "You're the only new friend I've made in a while. I'm glad you're going to the concert with me. You'll get to see a bit of what my life is like."

The only new friend. That's what he said. *The only new* friend. Did that mean that he really wasn't thinking of this thing as a date? If yes, it would make my life *so* much easier.

Of course, it might also make it harder to tell him I couldn't go. After all, he'd just told me I was his only new friend in ages. How could I ditch him after that?

You have to, a little voice in my mind told me. *You already have your feelings for Drew complicating things. You don't need a third guy mucking stuff up as well.*

I took a deep breath. This was not going to be fun.

"Ian, I—"

"Oh! Before I forget. Here. This is for you," Ian said, whipping something out of his messenger bag. He slapped it on the table and, once again, my jaw dropped.

"A backstage pass? A backstage pass?" I said, grabbing the laminated plastic up in my hands. "Are you *kidding* me?"

"We can watch the concert from there, or from the front row," he said. "Whatever you like."

"Does this mean we'll get to see their dressing rooms?"

"Yep. And we'll probably meet up with them before the show as well," Ian said. "They like to have a lot of fans around while they do their pre-show power circle. Something about positive energy."

Their power circle. I could be part of the Bloodworms's pre-show power circle. And then watch their concert from the wings. And then go to their party afterward where all kinds of famous people would probably show up.

"Are you excited?" Ian said.

"You have *no* idea," I said.

This was like a dream come true. I was going to hang with the Bloodworms. I was going to be the envy of every kid in school.

All I had to do was break Nate's heart to get there.

Nate was waiting for me by my locker after eighth period. Three guys in one day. I'm sure Debra Jack would have a few choice words if she heard about this.

"Hey," he said when he saw me. "Cara told me you came in late. Where were you this morning?"

What, did he think I went out with two other guys before the clock even hit one P.M.? Oh, right . . . I actually did do that.

"I was . . . uh . . . not feeling that well this morning," I said.

Liar! Stinking, awful liar!

"Are you okay?" he asked.

"Better now," I told him, swallowing a lump that had formed in my throat.

Lies, lies, lies!

"Good," he said. "I was worried about you."

I forced a smile. He was too sweet—and I was too evil.

"Well, I'd better get to practice," he said. "But I'm glad you're feeling better."

"Thanks. Me, too," I said.

He leaned in, gave me a quick kiss and a smile, and jogged away, leaving me feeling like the mud caked to the underside of my boot. With a sigh, I shoved a few things into my locker and headed for the *Reporter* office. When I walked in, everyone except for Mike was gathered around the same computer, whispering and laughing. Mike stood in the corner, red as a tomato, looking incredibly angry.

"What's up?" I asked.

Everyone turned around and half of them blanched. A few people moved guiltily away from the computer and all the little hairs on the back of my neck stood on end.

"What?" I said.

Jimmy Patel minimized the screen they had all been staring at.

"Nothing," he said. "Want to start the meeting?"

"Jimmy, what was on the screen when I walked in here?" I asked.

Jimmy looked around at our coworkers. Several of them looked away. Mike cleared his throat and stepped away from the wall.

"You're not gonna like it," Mike said.

"Oh, for God's sake."

I leaned over Jimmy, grabbed the mouse, and maximized the window. It was the forum. The fabulous Kensington Daze. Someone had made up a pretty cool-looking page with a fancy icon on top that read *Kensington High Hall of Shame*. Underneath was a picture of a bullfighter with the head of Mr. Suarez, one of the Spanish teachers, superimposed on the body. The caption beneath read: *Most Likely to Be Trampled to Death by Exiting Students Dying to Escape Boredom*.

It was someone's lame idea of a joke. Big freakin' deal. The next entry showed our principal digitally altered to look like Caesar in a toga. His award was: *Most Likely to*

Throw Students to the Lions.

It was stupid, but not freak-out worthy. Why was everyone acting so weird? I scrolled down and my heart stopped. There was my senior picture, digitally placed atop the body of an obvious street-walker. Underneath it was the caption: *Most Likely to Give It Up to Anyone and Everyone.*

nine

"Look. We have two choices," Cara said, leaning forward in her chair. She had arrived at *The Reporter* about two seconds after my total humiliation and taken charge of the situation. Which, as of now, meant turning off all the computers so I wouldn't be able to stare at that horrifying posting and obsess. "We either leave the stuff as is, or we take down the whole site. We can't pick and choose what stays up there, because people will freak. And besides, it's not like any of us has the time to sit around and edit it."

"But if we take it all down, we risk losing about half our readership *and* our advertising dollars," Anna remarked. She looked at me apologetically. "Just playing devil's advocate."

"It's okay," I said.

"I don't know about you guys, but right now I don't even care," Cara said. "It's not just Layla. There are tons of kids getting torn down on that thing."

"What do you think, Layla?" Mike asked.

"I don't know," I said, my mind still reeling over the awful image of me as a prostitute. "Can I at least find out who's trashing me? Maybe we can turn them in to the principal or something and, I don't know, make an example out of them. Maybe that'll make people think twice about what they post."

"There's no way to tell for sure," Mike said. "The posts are anonymous, and most of them trace back to the computer lab."

I sighed and sat back in my seat. I couldn't believe that someone would do something like this. Even evil Debra Jack, who was, at that point, my prime suspect. What did she possibly have to gain from making me look like a whore? Did she really think that was going to make Nate like her?

"I need to think about it," I said finally.

"Layla," Cara protested. "Come on."

"Cara, I'm not going to sit here and whine about people spreading false rumors about me," I said, then looked around at the rest of the staff. "And they *are* false in case anyone was curious."

"But it's not just you," Cara said. "What about everyone else who's getting trashed?"

"I know, but if it means losing half our budget—"

"Layla—"

"Let's just think about it," I repeated. "We'll figure it out by next week."

Cara sighed. "If that's what you want."

What I really wanted was to get the heck out of there, go home, and go directly to bed.

"That's what I want," I said. "So, meeting adjourned."

Friday morning Cara's car was still in the shop, so my mother drove me to school. When I got out of the car at the front of the school, Anna was waiting for me, looking tense.

Oh, God. What had they posted now? "Hey, Anna. What's up?" I asked.

"I think I may know who put up the *Kensington High Hall of Shame*," she said, glancing over her shoulder. She fished around in her bag and pulled out a tattered, folded piece of white, lined paper. "I found this on the floor in French class yesterday."

I unfolded the page to find a crude drawing of me in an extremely compromising position with the words *Layla— Most Likely to Give It Up to Anyone and Everyone* underneath it.

Below the drawing was a note in girly handwriting.

H: What do you think? I wanna put it up at lunch.

Then, in different handwriting, the reply.

D: You are too funny. Nate will never slum again after this.

D and *H*. My throat went dry as my suspicions were confirmed. So Debra Jack and her back end, Hannah, were behind this after all. Why was I not surprised?

"Thanks, Anna," I said, shoving the paper into my bag.

"Just don't tell them it was me who gave that to you," she said nervously. "Last year they had it in for *me*, remember? I still have the scars."

"Don't worry," I said, thinking back to the nasty rumors about Anna's nonexistent eating disorder.

"So, what're you gonna do?" she asked.

"Get them back," I said blithely. "And I'll make sure you're around when I do it."

Anna smiled and together, we made our way into school.

The entire day, every time I walked into a room, all conversation would cease instantly. I caught more than a few amused looks and overheard a ton of giggles. Everyone was talking about the *Kensington High Hall of Shame* and I was the star.

Not exactly the kind of spotlight a girl hopes for.

Luckily Ian was absent, probably playing hooky to hang out with the band and help his dad, so his ears were safe from all the gossip for the moment. And Nate acted completely normal all day, as if he hadn't heard a thing. How that was possible, I had no idea, but I wasn't about to question it. I just wanted to get through Friday.

Of course that would lead to Saturday and I still hadn't made a decision about what I was doing Saturday night. Maybe I could just crawl under a rock somewhere and wait for a few years to pass me by. That would pretty much solve everything.

I managed to keep my head high most of the day, but by eighth period it was getting a little old and I was getting a little exhausted. Plus, just to add insult to injury, I was going to have to take the bus home. After last bell I ducked into the bathroom so that I wouldn't have to suffer through the many stops squirming around with my legs crossed. At this point, even the smallest comfort was going to help.

I was just about to leave my stall when the bathroom door opened. Instantly I recognized the voices of Missy Tyler and Erica Sherman, two more members of Debra's bitch squad.

"So, what's it gonna be? The purple or the red?" Missy asked.

I heard the sound of a backpack being propped up on the counter and a few zippers being undone. They were in for a complete makeup session.

Great. I could either go out there and deal with more stares and snarky comments, or I could wait it out. Normally I would have gone with option A, but I'd had a long day already. I lowered the lid, sat down quietly, and pulled my feet up.

"The purple, definitely," Erica answered. "Everyone's gonna be wearing red."

"I wonder what Layla Carter's gonna wear. Fishnets and a thong?" Missy suggested.

Erica laughed. My jaw dropped open. Didn't anyone around here have anything else to talk about?

"I still cannot believe Nate is taking her," Erica said.

"What did she do, brainwash him?"

"Must have. I heard from Debra that Connie Ralston saw Layla having lunch with that new British kid at Pizza Pizza the other day," Missy told her. "She's totally cheating on Nate."

Oh my God. Oh crap, crap, crap.

"No, no, no. It's not Ian, it's Drew Sullivan," Erica corrected.

Wha-huh?

"Excuse me?" Missy said.

"She's cheating on Nate with Drew Sullivan," Erica said. "I saw her on the back of his bike the other day. And everyone knows Drew doesn't let you on the back of his bike unless he's getting something out of it, if you know what I mean."

I felt like I was going to throw up. At least, I was in the perfect place for it. That was something.

"Omigod. That is so unfair. She gets to have Nate Henry *and* Drew Sullivan?" Missy said. "What is she, like, some kind of witch?"

"Or a black widow," Erica said. "Omigod, maybe she's going out with Ian, too. Maybe she's sleeping with all three of them!" she suggested gleefully.

"Wouldn't put it past her," Missy said. "God, what a major ho."

"Tell me about it. I'm glad Debra put that thing up on the Daze. She deserves it," Erica replied. "Come on. We're gonna be late for practice."

"I can't believe Nate hasn't broken up with her yet, with

all these rumors floating around," Missy said.

"He will soon, if Debra has anything to say about it," Erica replied, heading for the door. "I'll bet you my entire MAC lip-gloss collection that those two do not show up at the dance together tomorrow night. When Debra sets her mind to something . . ."

"Your entire collection?" Missy said. "Oh, you are so on."

Two seconds later the door swung open and I was left in the bathroom in silence, trying to catch my breath and keep from hurling all at once. I couldn't believe people had seen me with both Ian and Drew. What was I going to do?

I needed air. Like, now.

I grabbed my bag and ran out of the bathroom, nearly running Nate down in the hallway.

"Hey! What's going on?" he asked, steadying me with his hands.

"Nothing. I have to go," I told him.

Nate looked at me, his expression serious. "Actually, I was hoping we could talk."

Oh, God. He'd heard. He was going to break up with me. No one had ever broken up with me before. And the first one was going to be Nate Henry? One of the very few guys I actually *wanted* to be with?

I don't *think* so!

"I'm sorry. I can't right now," I said, still on the move. "I'll . . . call you later."

"Layla—"

"I have to go!" I shouted, on the verge of tears.

Then I turned and ran before any of my classmates could see me and think *they* were the ones who had caused the breakdown.

ten

By the time I had stormed my way to the bus shelter, the tears were gone and I was pissed. I hated Debra Jack. Completely and utterly hated her. What was her problem, anyway? She always had to be attacking someone. Last year she had spread all these rumors that Anna had an eating disorder and that she was being forced to spend lunch in the nurse's office so they could make sure she was eating. The year before that she had totally destroyed one of her supposed best friends, Jordana Thacker, by getting everyone to believe that she'd gotten pregnant by a guy who wasn't her boyfriend and had gone away all summer to have the baby.

All of it was untrue, but everyone always believed her because she based her fictions on things that *could* be true.

Anna was, after all, extremely thin and Jordana had gained weight and broken up with her boyfriend, so the rumors played right into the facts.

The girl had a great future in the tabloids.

But this time, she had messed with the wrong girl. She couldn't just decide when my relationship with Nate was going to be over. That was *my* decision.

And a decision I was going to have to make soon. Valentine's Day was less than ten hours away.

After a few minutes of watching my breath make steam clouds, the bus finally arrived. I climbed aboard and settled into one of the front seats. Two seconds later, my cell phone rang.

The little old woman across from me shot me an irritated look. I dug my phone out quickly. It was Nate. A sliver of fear shot through me. Guess waiting until tonight to break up with me was too long. I turned the phone off and tossed it back in my bag.

The bus stopped short at a clogged intersection near the center of town and I groaned. I just wanted to get home, crawl under my covers, and hide from the world for a while. A rock, after all, was a tad unrealistic.

Frustrated, I gazed out the window at the stream of cars in front of the bus. I noticed someone on a motorcycle, weaving in and out of the stopped traffic.

Lucky guy, I thought.

Then I realized the bike was red. A red Norton.

I couldn't believe it. It was like fate was trying to send me a sign. Screw the high school boys and all the stupid rumors. Clearly the world was trying to bring me and Drew Sullivan together.

Down the block, Drew swerved and pulled into a parking space. He got off his bike and cut across the street quickly, looking harried. Where was he going in such a hurry?

Suddenly all my Drew-stalker tendencies from a couple of years ago kicked in. I was intrigued. I had to know what he was up to.

And besides, it would take my mind off all my issues, at least for a little while.

There was a bus stop at the next corner. As we edged closer and closer I kept my eye on Drew. He was headed for a nearby strip mall.

"Come on . . . come on," I said under my breath, my heart pounding. We passed by another bus, which blocked Drew from sight. "Dammit," I muttered.

Another dirty look from the old lady.

"Don't worry. I'm getting off," I told her.

She huffed and turned away. Finally the bus stopped and the airbrakes hissed. The second the door opened I was out. I raced to the back of the bus and looked across the street. Drew was nowhere to be seen.

"Crap."

I turned for the bus again, but it was already taking off. Sure. *Now* it moves. I would have to wait for the next one. What was *wrong* with me? Why did Drew have such an insane affect on me?

Slowly, I strolled toward the parked Norton. Even without Drew on its back, the bike was hot. God, it would be so cool to date Drew. This could be my boyfriend's bike.

Yeah, my boyfriend rides a Norton.

So sweet.

Of course, who knew if Drew had any interest at all in dating me? That forehead kiss had been kind of brotherly. Maybe he was trying to blow me off.

Why did boys have to be so confusing?

A gust of cold wind blew right through my cute but extremely impractical brown leather, mini bomber jacket, and I really started to regret getting off the bus. It would be at least ten minutes until the next one came by, so I decided to pop into the Starbucks on the corner for a hot chocolate while I waited. As I turned, a flash of white next to the Norton's front tire caught my eye—a neatly folded piece of paper.

Curious, I picked it up. Inside the fold was an intricate drawing of a dragon wrapped in a thorny rosebush. Drew's signature was scrawled on the bottom right-hand corner. I had seen Drew's work in school art shows and always loved it, but this drawing was better than anything he'd ever done before. Way better. And he'd lost it on the street.

I had to get this back to him. But how? There was no way I could just leave it on his bike. It would blow away in about two-point-five seconds. And I didn't know where he lived. Should I just wait there until he came back?

I squinted at the timer on the meter. He'd paid for two hours. No way. I'd freeze my butt off.

Okay. Veronica Mars time. Where, in the immediate vicinity, would Drew have gone? I checked out the stores on the main drag: Urban Outfitters, Progressive Books, Toys of Wonder, Aldo's restaurant, Vinny's Tattoo Palace. . . .

Bingo. I looked at the drawing again. This could definitely be a tattoo design. Vinny's was as good a spot as any to start.

Clutching the paper, I crossed the street and headed right for the tattoo place. My pulse raced in my veins. How was I going to explain this to Drew, exactly?

Hey, I was stalking you and I found your drawing?

Yeah, right. Apparently I would just have to wing it.

When I stepped into Vinny's a set of door chimes just like my mom's tinkled above my head and I almost laughed. Guess people were more alike than I thought.

Vinny's was surprisingly clean and well lit. *Palace* it was not, however. The front room consisted mainly of a long display case that held a variety of rings, jeweled studs, and U-shaped jewelry that I assumed were for piercings. Behind the case were framed photos of people showing off their body art. On the far side of the room was what seemed like a waiting area—a leather sectional sofa and a glass coffee table covered with a bunch of tattoo-related magazines. A disturbingly real-looking zebra skin was draped over the back of the couch. Across from the waiting area hung a purple curtain, which I guessed led to where the tattoos and piercings were done.

Drew was nowhere in sight.

"Help you?" asked the burly, bald, heavily tattooed man behind the counter.

"Um, just looking. Thanks."

I walked casually over to the waiting area, grabbed a magazine, and pretended to look through it for ideas. What the hell was I doing here? I was going to look like such a loser when I ended up ducking out. But what was I going to do, get a tat just so burly man wouldn't think I was a wuss? Hardly.

"Dammit. It was right here. It must have fallen out or something."

My heart stopped. That was Drew's voice. It was coming from behind a curtain just a few feet away.

"We can't work without it," another man answered.

Drew cursed under his breath. "I know that. That design took weeks."

The dragon. He had to be looking for the dragon. Screwing up all my courage, I dropped the magazine and started for the curtain. At that moment it was whipped aside and suddenly, I was face to face with Drew.

"Layla," he said, understandably surprised.

Just hearing him say my name gave me goose bumps all over.

"Hey," I said casually.

Drew looked around as if searching for a hidden camera. "What're you doing here?"

"I . . . I'm looking for a tattoo?" I said.

"Nice," Drew said approvingly.

I grinned. He thought I was cool.

"Are you getting one?" I asked.

Drew sighed. "I was going to, but I lost my design."

Practically trembling, I held up the sketch. "Is this it?" I asked.

Drew's eyes widened and he snatched the paper from my hand. "Where did you get this?"

"I . . . uh . . . found it on the way in," I lied.

"Layla, you have no idea . . . " he said, excited. "Thank you."

"You're welcome," I said giddily.

I heard a grunt and turned to look at the burly man. He shook his head at us as he flipped through a magazine and I flushed. Apparently my crush was obvious to the world.

"Dude. I got it," Drew said, heading back toward the curtain.

Obvious to everyone but Drew. Unless, of course, he was choosing to ignore it.

My heart was just starting its downward spiral into disappointment when Drew paused and turned to look at me. "Hey, do you want to stay and watch him do this?"

"You mean watch you get a tattoo?" I asked, feeling both disbelief and excitement.

Drew swallowed and for the briefest of seconds, looked sheepish. "I could probably use the support."

You couldn't have wiped the grin off my face with a hundred thousand official *Kensington High Hall of Shame* erasers. Drew Sullivan needed me. He was asking for my help.

"I'd love to stay."

"God, this hurts," Drew said.

He clenched his teeth as his buddy Tom, a bald guy with body art everywhere, touched the needle to his arm again. Drew was kicked back in a long, leather, dentist-style chair, shirtless, while I sat in a wooden folding chair in the corner. It was all I could do to keep from salivating at his perfectly chiseled chest. Of course the buzz of the needle and the blood and the obvious pain were pretty good distractions.

"First tat is always the hardest," Tom said.

I winced as blood trickled along Drew's skin. This hardly looked worth it.

"Talk to your girlfriend," Tom said. "It helps to put your mind on something else."

My heart skipped a half dozen beats at the mention of the word *girlfriend*. Drew, however, didn't seem to notice.

"Okay, so, Layla," he said with some effort. "What're you doing this weekend?"

Oh, any number of things, I thought. *Dances, concerts, parties . . .* But Drew didn't need to know I already had dueling dates.

"Not much," I said evasively. The needle buzzed and Drew groaned. "You?" I asked, looking away.

"Actually, I have an art show," Drew said, taking a deep breath and holding it. "This gallery's gonna show some of my work."

"Really? That's great," I said, suddenly breathless myself.

"Yeah. It's a real opportunity for me," Drew said, then

turned his head to the side with a grimace as some more blood appeared.

"Just don't get too high-and-mighty," Tom said, leaning in to study his work. "I still want you working for us."

"I know, man," Drew said.

"You want to be a tattoo artist?" I asked, perplexed.

"He wouldn't be doing this," Tom said, adjusting his seat. "Just designing. My boss Crabbe pays real good for new designs."

"It's a way to pay the bills," Drew explained. "But I gotta do a few more examples before he gives me the job."

"Oh. That's cool," I said. "People will be walking around with your artwork on them. Like live billboards."

Drew laughed through the pain. "Exactly."

Finally, after what seemed like forever, Tom was done. Drew sat up with a wince and Tom taped gauze over the tat. Instantly dots of blood appeared everywhere. Ouch.

"So. What are we doing for you?" Tom said, turning to me.

"What?" I said, stunned.

"A heart? A moon? Angels are really popular with the ladies."

"Um . . ."

"It'll be on me. For staying," Drew said, gingerly pulling his T-shirt over his head. "You said you were getting one, right?"

Nice one, Layla. How about controlling that big mouth of yours?

"Um, I'm not really sure what I want," I said. "I need to think about it some more, you know? It's a big decision since it's gonna be there for, well, forever."

Tom and Drew exchanged a patronizing look that made my blood boil. They thought I was chickening out. That I was afraid of a little pain.

Well, they were right. But they didn't have to know that.

"How about a piercing?" I suggested. "I've always thought about doing my navel."

At least that was true. Of course, my mother had forbidden it several times over.

"Sweet," Drew said, glancing at my covered stomach in a way that made me blush.

"Let's do it," Tom said.

Ten minutes later I had picked out a small gold ring with a tiny sparkly charm dangling from it. I brought it back to Tom, and he sterilized it, then laid it next to his shiny tools, some of which looked pretty freakin' scary.

"Okay. On the table," Tom said.

I swallowed back a huge lump of fear and climbed on, laying down on my back. Drew stood next to me and gave me an encouraging look. Part of me still couldn't believe we were doing this together. Me and Drew Sullivan, getting tattoos and piercings.

I was such a rebel.

"I'm gonna need to see your belly button," Tom said coaxingly.

"Oh. Right. Sorry." I lifted my shirt.

Tom leaned in with a long, scary-looking silver instrument.

"Wait!" I automatically reached for Drew's hand. He looked surprised at first and I instantly regretted it, but then he tightened his grip and stepped a little closer to me. A rush of gratitude warmed me from head to toe.

"Don't worry," Drew said. "You're gonna be fine."

I smiled and squeezed his hand.

"Okay, go," I told Tom.

Tom grinned. He liked doing this a little too much. He clamped down my belly button with the instrument, then pulled it out.

"Ow!" I cried, staring at my stretched navel.

"This is the worst part," he assured me, but somehow I didn't believe him. Then in one quick swoop he stabbed right through the skin with a thick needle. The pain was excruciating.

"Ugh!"

Drew and I winced in unison at that one.

"Get it out! Get it out!" I shouted.

An instant later he snapped in my jewelry, and I was done.

"See? That wasn't so bad," Tom said.

My stomach throbbed like a tiny boxer was trying to punch his way out of my gut. I sat up gingerly and looked down at my belly button. It was all angry and red, but the jewelry was kind of cute.

"Wow," I said. I couldn't believe I had actually

gone through with it.

"I'll be right back with the antiseptic and stuff," Tom said, ducking out.

I swung my legs over the side of the table and Drew stepped closer to me, staring down at my stomach. My heart pounded at his closeness.

"Damn," he said. "That's sexy."

I grinned up at him. "Yeah?"

"Yeah," he said, his voice husky.

Then, just like that, he'd slipped his hands under my hair and we were kissing. Kissing like our lives depended on it.

My fingers gripped his T-shirt as his tongue toyed with mine. This was no forehead kiss and quick dismissal. This was perfection.

Apparently sharing traumatic experiences was very romantic.

"Layla," he whispered, breaking away. "Come to my show with me tomorrow," he said quietly, still holding my face in his hands. "I want you to see my work."

My mind was fuzzy with pain and excitement. He wanted to share his work with me! He wanted to spend the most exciting night of his artistic life with me!

I nodded quickly. All I wanted was to feel his lips on mine again. "I'm there," I said.

"Good," he kissed me quickly once more. "I'll pick you up at seven."

Seven . . . seven. . . . Why did that sound familiar? My muddled mind was just about to land on it when Tom returned with a bottle of antiseptic and a sheet of instructions on how to care for my piercing.

It wasn't until Drew had dropped me at home and I turned on my phone and saw that I had several messages from both Nate and Ian that I remembered.

Seven. Tomorrow. Yeah. I already had two dates.

Nice one, Layla. Nice one.

eleven

"Cara, I need you to get over here. Like, now," I said into the phone.

It was Saturday. Valentine's Day. And it was already three o'clock. I had become the master procrastinator with a gold medal in avoiding phone calls. All it had taken was a couple of e-mails to Nate and Ian the night before, telling them I couldn't call back because I wasn't feeling well, and the phone had miraculously stopped ringing. I was a big, fat, liar. That was what a girl had to do when she was incapable of making decisions. And I was definitely incapable. Thus, the panicked phone call.

"What's wrong?" she asked.

"What's wrong? What's *wrong*?" I shouted, pacing my room in my bathrobe. Laid out on my bed were three outfits: Simple, sexy black dress for Nate, ripped jeans and tank for Ian, black pants and sophisticated top for Drew. I had no idea which one I would be wearing. "What's wrong is I have three dates getting here in four hours."

"Three . . . three what?" Cara said weakly. "Wait a minute, I thought it was two."

"It *was* two," I said, throwing up my hand. "Until Drew asked me to his gallery opening yesterday and I said yes."

"Layla! Why? Why did you say yes?"

"Because! It was Drew Sullivan! And he kissed me! And I'd just . . . gotten a belly button piercing and I think all the adrenaline was messing with my brain," I said, putting my hand over my eyes and sitting down on my desk chair.

"You got a *what*? All right. That's it. I'll be right there."

The line went dead and I got up and flopped facedown on my bed on top of my jeans. Pain shot through my stomach and I flipped over, cursing my own stupidity.

How had I let it get this far? How, how, how?

"Okay, let's think about this logically," Cara said as I watched the minute hand on the kitchen clock move up a notch. Cara had shown up in her red V-Day dress, all coiffed and ready to go, her curly hair falling in sweet tendrils around her face. "You have to go with Nate. It's obvious."

"You only want me to go with Nate because then I'll be going to the dance with you," I said, leaning my elbows on the counter. "Besides, we don't know for sure that Nate even wants to go with me. He may have already heard all about me and Ian and me and Drew. I swear he was trying to break up with me yesterday."

"You don't know that for sure," Cara said, pointing her finger at me.

"Call it women's intuition," I said grumpily.

"All right, so then it's Ian," Cara said with a shrug. "I mean, the guy is offering backstage passes to the Bloodworms and the potential to party with Necro. Hello? You've been fantasizing about that since fifth grade."

"I know. But is it really fair to pick him because of what he can give me?" I said. "Isn't that kind of like using him?"

"Well . . . how do you feel about him?" Cara asked.

"I'm definitely attracted to him, but I'm not sure," I said, feeling desperate. "It might just be the mystique."

Cara groaned. "Okay, fine. Go with Drew then. God, you've wanted Drew since you were a zygote. It's totally obvious. Why are we even discussing this?"

"Because Nate is ridiculously sweet and Ian is ridiculously hot and exotic and I am just going to kill myself," I said, standing up. "So, what do you suggest I do, then?" I said.

"I suggest you be a woman," Cara said firmly, standing up straight and crossing her arms over her chest. "It's tough love time, my friend. I'm sorry, but you got yourself into this mess, Layla. Now you have to get yourself out of it. So decide. Who's it gonna be? The jock, the Brit, or the lifelong crush?"

"I don't know!" I wailed.

"Well you'd better decide and you'd better do it now," Cara said, glancing grimly at the clock. "Cuz you officially have less than an hour before your driveway is overflowing with guys. And that just ain't gonna be pretty."

The Choice

Okay, Cara's right. In less than an hour there's gonna be a rumble in the driveway unless I do something now. But I am clearly incapable of making up my own mind. Yeah, I like to have my fun, but this past week has been too psychotic to be considered fun. It's time for me to focus on one guy. So I'm leaving it up to you. Who's it gonna be?

1. Nate

Pros: He's totally gorgeous and sweet and he makes me light up whenever I see him. Plus, he really cares about me and not about his image. And there's the added bonus of the fact that my being with him clearly drives Debra Jack crazy.

Cons: He may or may not want to break up with me
already. Plus, he's not my usual type. What if I get
bored?

Risk of heartbreak: Significant—for both of us.

· ·

2. Ian

Pros: There's obviously the Bloodworms pull, but there's
also that indescribable chemistry between us. I
cannot stop flirting with him even when I try!

Cons: I know next to nothing about him. Except for the
fact that his girlfriend ditched him only two weeks
after he left the country. Is he a bad boyfriend?

Risk of heartbreak: Moderate—even if this is just for fun.

· ·

3. Drew

Pros: Hot, hot, hottie. His kisses pretty much melt me.
He's older, ridiculously sexy, and definitely mysterious.
Plus, I've been crushing on him since sophomore
year and now I finally have my shot. How could I
pass that up?

Cons: Does he really like me, or does he just like to kiss me?
It's next to impossible to tell with his cool demeanor.

Risk of heartbreak: Hefty—if he's playing with me, I'll be
crushed.

· ·

Well, there you have it. My happiness is in your hands. Choose wisely!

If you choose *Nate,*
keep reading.

If you choose *Ian,*
turn to page 153.

If you choose *Drew,*
turn to page 203.

You Chose Nate

twelve

"Okay. I'm going with Nate," I said finally. I felt a little thrill as I made the decision, accompanied by a wave of doubt. I wanted to be with Nate. I really did. But what if he didn't want to be with me?

"Yay!" Cara jumped up and down in her fluffy dress, looking like a pixie on speed.

"Yeah. Let's just hope he still wants me," I said, my heart fluttering with nervousness.

"He does! He does! Don't worry," Cara said, grabbing my arm and dragging me toward the stairs. "Come on! Let's get you dressed."

"Wait. I have to make a couple of phone calls first," I said, swallowing hard.

Cara grimaced. "Oh, right. Forgot about that part.

Want me to stay for moral support?"

"Nah. I think I'd rather do this alone. Why don't you go pick out my makeup or something?" I suggested.

Cara grabbed me up in a hug. "Good luck. I'm upstairs if you need me."

"Thanks," I said.

I picked up my cell from the counter and dialed Ian first. He picked up on the first ring.

"Lay-la-la!" he sang. "Are you ready to party?"

I bit my lip. "Actually, Ian, I'm really sorry but I'm not gonna be able to make it."

"What? Why?" he asked.

"I kind of have a Valentine's Day date. With my boyfriend," I said, squeezing my eyes closed.

"Hold on. You have a boyfriend?" he snapped. He sounded surprised. Really, truly surprised, which in a way surprised me. "Since when?"

"Since always," I said, feeling awful.

"Unbelievable." His tone went from surprise to anger in no time. "So, what? You were leading me on all this time? Using me for the ticket?"

"No! We never said it was a date!" I said, grasping at straws. "You called me your friend! I thought—"

"Oh, please, Layla. You are not that naïve," Ian said. "Well, fine then. Have a lovely date with your *boy*friend. I hope you know you just missed out on what would have been the best night of your life. I'll give Necro my best for you."

And just like that, the line went dead.

Right. Okay. That went well. What a class-A jerk. He hadn't even tried to be understanding. Guess I dodged a bullet there.

I scrolled down to Drew's number, which he had programmed in my phone the day before. I only hoped he would take the news a bit better.

"I can't believe it. He actually sounded disappointed. Drew Sullivan, disappointed that I, Layla Carter, was telling him no," I whispered, as I perched on the couch in my black dress.

"Damn. You have powers you didn't even know you had," Cara said.

"Tell me about it."

At least Drew had taken it better than Ian had, possibly because he had been in the middle of what sounded like a pretty rocking pre-art show party, and now I had no regrets. I was going to focus on Nate and only Nate. If only he would show up already.

"Don't worry. He's not officially late yet," Cara said.

"What're you, a mind reader?"

Cara shrugged. "It's a gift."

My heart flipped over when I heard the telltale closing of a car door in the driveway.

"He's here!"

Cara and I both knelt on the couch as I pushed aside the curtain and looked out. Nate was just getting out of his car looking beyond gorgeous in a charcoal gray suit.

"He's wearing a suit! That's a good sign," I said.

He lifted out a bouquet of roses from the passenger seat.

"And he's got flowers!" Cara added. "A guy who wants to break up with you before a dance does not wear a suit and bring flowers."

Mike, who had come over a little earlier and had been hanging out in the kitchen watching the Knicks game on the mini TV for the past fifteen minutes, walked in behind us.

"What're you two doing?" he asked, looking suspicious.

"Nothing!" I trilled, jumping up. I smoothed my dress and licked my teeth to clear any stray lipstick.

"I guess he didn't hear the rumors," I whispered to Cara.

"Or maybe he just chooses not to believe them," Cara said. "Maybe he chooses to trust you."

I grinned. I liked that idea even better. Except that some of the rumors—some of them—were true. So technically, if Nate was choosing to trust me, he was choosing wrong.

The doorbell rang and I took a deep breath.

That was all in the past. From now on, it was just Nate. From now on, he *could* trust me. I was officially a one-man girl.

I walked over to the door and opened it. Nate flushed when he saw me.

"Layla . . . wow," he said, looking me up and down. "I mean, wow."

I grinned. "Wow is good."

He looked into my eyes. "Wow is *definitely* good."

"Well, wow yourself," I said. "Are those for me?"

Nate stared when he looked at the flowers as if he'd completely forgotten they were there. "Oh! Yeah! Happy Valentine's Day. And anniversary."

"Thanks. You, too," I said. I leaned in and gave him a long, lingering kiss. When I finally pulled back, it took a moment for his eyes to open. "Come on in. I'll put these in water."

I heard Nate greeting Mike and Cara as I fished a vase out of the cabinet and added some water. Suddenly, I realized my hands were trembling and I stopped for a moment and told myself to chill.

Nate was here. He still wanted to be with me. Debra had not, as Erica had predicted, ruined everything for me. And I was not going to let her.

I placed the roses in water, grabbed my coat and purse, and headed back to the living room.

"Come on," I said, slipping my arm through Nate's. "Suddenly, I feel like dancing."

When we arrived at the school, the parking lot was crammed with kids heading toward the building. Nate took my hand and a sizzle of anticipation raced through me. My first school dance. Call me cheesy, but I was totally psyched.

Inside a pathway of red and pink rose petals led to the gym door, which was surrounded by a gaudy white and pink lattice. We paused under a swag of pink and red balloons and Cara and I both laughed.

"Whoa. They really outdid themselves, huh?" Nate said, slipping my coat from my shoulders.

"It looks like Cupid threw up in here," I said.

Nate laughed and I blushed with pleasure.

"Nice imagery, Carter," Mike said.

"Come on," Nate said, tugging on my hand. "If it's this bad out here, imagine what it's like in there."

Okay, actually, it was kind of pretty inside. The gym had been completely transformed. Red hearts covered the walls and white twinkling lights were strung everywhere. Thousands of balloons crowded the ceiling with silver and red metallic ribbons hanging down from the sky. Tables surrounded the dance floor, covered with more rose petals and red and pink cupid confetti.

"There's our table," Nate said, lifting his chin toward the back of the room.

"We're gonna go put our stuff down," I told Cara. "Be right back."

Nate steered me through the maze of tables to one on the far side of the gym where his friends Oliver and Darren were hovering, chatting animatedly about basketball, most likely. As we arrived, one of the chaperones moved out of my way and I saw the guys' dates seated at the table. I almost tripped.

It was Missy and Erica.

Classic.

"Oh, hello girls," I said with a sly smile. I placed my bag down on a chair and leaned my hands into it. "Love the purple dress, Erica. Good choice."

They both just gaped at me in shock.

"Uh . . . thanks," Erica said finally.

"That's MAC lip gloss you're wearing, right?" I said, loving every minute of this. "Shouldn't you be handing that over to Missy right about now?"

The two of them looked at one another, totally snagged. Then Erica pushed herself up from the table and grabbed her purse.

"I have to go to the bathroom," she said.

Missy got up to follow.

"Yeah. Check under the stalls this time," I said under my breath.

They both shot me looks of death before scurrying off.

"What was that about?" Nate asked me, his hand warm on my shoulder.

"Oh, just a little personal joke," I said, turning around to face him. "Come on. Let's dance."

A couple of hours later we had eaten dinner and I felt happy and full and completely and utterly sure of my choice. Dancing with Nate was even better than I had daydreamed it would be. He smelled amazing, like fabric softener and spicy soap, and the way he held me close made me feel . . . special. No one had ever made me feel so special before.

"This is the best Valentine's Day ever," I said, resting my head on his shoulder as we swayed to a slow song.

"Definitely," he replied, giving me a little squeeze.

I looked up dreamily and my eyes fell on Debra Jack.

She was standing on the periphery of the dance floor in a seriously slinky aqua dress, with Hannah, Missy, and Erica around her, basically staring me down. She whispered something to Hannah and narrowed her eyes at me. Instantly my heart rate sped up. What was that girl planning next? Was she just going to come over here and tell Nate point blank that I'd been cheating on him?

"Feel like getting out of here?" Nate suddenly whispered in my ear.

I smiled at his perfect timing. "You have no idea."

We grabbed our coats, said good-bye to Cara and to Nate's friends, and headed for the lobby. Out of the corner of my eye I saw Debra watching us and I could have sworn she made a move to follow. This girl was obsessed. I was really starting to think that Cara was right. She definitely wanted Nate for herself. It was the only explanation for her all-out behavior.

I couldn't get Nate out of there fast enough.

"Hang on a sec," Nate said, pausing in the lobby. He touched his pockets. "Did I leave my cell phone back there?"

I saw a flash of aqua blue on the other side of the open door and panicked. I grabbed Nate by the lapel and pulled him right into the boys' bathroom. Instantly the one kid at the far urinal zipped up and ran out as fast as his feet could carry him.

"Layla! What the heck are you doing?" Nate asked, completely stunned.

"I have to ask you something," I said, leaning back

against the side of the nearest stall. The metal was cool and comforting on my hot skin.

"Okay," he said, looking at me like I was nuts. "But you do realize this is the boys' room."

"Yeah. But I have to ask you this now or I'm going to go crazy, and I don't want Debra and her posse walking in on us," I said.

"Oh. Well then you picked the perfect place."

He still looked confused. Not that I could blame him. I pushed myself away from the wall and sighed.

"I'm not really sure how to ask this," I said, glancing at him warily.

"Just ask," Nate said. He looked so unsuspecting, I almost chickened out completely. But I couldn't live like this any longer, knowing that at any second the roof might cave in.

"I was just wondering if you've, I don't know, *read* anything about me recently," I said quickly.

Nate's face was unreadable. I felt my pulse speed up exponentially in the two seconds before he started to speak.

"Honestly? Yeah," he said, and paused.

Oh, God. What was he thinking? I couldn't handle the silence. "And?"

"Look, people can be mean." Nate stared directly into my eyes. "And people talk trash, too. But I like you. I trust you . . . and I want to get to know *you*. I don't care what other people think they know."

Wow. Could he have possibly said anything more perfect?

I tried to swallow the lump that had lodged itself in the center of my throat. I don't think I fully understood until that moment how much Nate respected me . . . and how much I liked him. Maybe it was because I'd never let a guy truly get under my skin before. But the more time I spent with Nate, the more I realized that Nate had been the only choice all along—the only one I really *wanted* to be with.

"How about this," he said, putting his arms around my waist. "How about we just pretend the rest of this stupid school doesn't exist? It's just you and me."

"That sounds like perfection," I said, melting against him.

"Good," Nate said. He glanced behind him at the door. "Now, I would kiss you, but that's not exactly something I've ever wanted to do in a boys' room."

I laughed and together we walked out the door. Debra was standing right next to the school exit, looking determined. A few of her friends had gathered around her, just salivating for a scene. My heart caught with fear for a split second.

Debra stepped forward as we approached. "Hey, Nate! I need to tell you some—"

"Sorry, Debra," Nate said, throwing up a hand as we walked right by her. "I don't care."

The look on her face was so classic it was going to be burned on my brain forever. All her friends laughed, hiding their mirth badly behind their hands. At that moment I knew I didn't have to get her back for the *Hall of Shame*.

Nate had just done it for me. I wished Anna had been there to see it.

As we twirled out into the darkness, I pulled him to me for a kiss. My knight in a charcoal gray suit.

thirteen

Normally, I hated Mondays just like the rest of the sane world, but on the Monday after Valentine's Day, I walked into school grinning like a moron. My weekend with Nate had been complete perfection, and I had actually made it to a one-month anniversary. On top of being extraordinarily happy, I was kind of proud of myself, I must say.

Then, I saw Ian waiting for me by my locker and my stomach took a dip. What was he doing there? Did he want to tell me off all over again?

"Hello," I said coolly, going right for my lock.

"Hey, Lay-la-la," he sang. "How was *your* weekend?"

I looked at him, confused. What was he on? Did he not remember how rude he was to me the last time we spoke?

"It was fabulous, actually," I said. "Yours?"

He sucked in a breath through his teeth and smiled. "Well, you missed a bloody good show on Saturday."

I felt a pang of jealousy, but let it pass. There would be other Bloodworms concerts. There was only one Nate and only one one-month anniversary. I pulled a few books out of my locker and shook my hair back blithely.

"I'm glad you had fun," I said.

"It would have been more fun if you had been there," Ian said huskily, moving closer to me.

Okay, step back. What was up with this guy? Was he schizo or something? My heart pounded with nervousness as I glanced over my shoulder. What if somebody misinterpreted what they were seeing and told Nate? What if *Nate* saw us?

"Uh, Ian, aren't you forgetting something?" I said, my face growing warm.

"What's that, love?" he asked with a sly smile.

I slammed my locker door and turned to him, hoping he'd pick up on the seriously negative body language. "Uh, how about the fact that I have a boyfriend?" I said. "Or the fact that you were a complete ass to me on Saturday."

Ian laughed, tipping his head back. "First of all, I think you were the one who blew me off at the last minute. But I'm willing to forgive that. Secondly, you and Mr. All American are not going to last."

My mouth dropped open. "Excuse me?"

"Come on, Layla. That git is about as fun as a chemistry quiz. Forget him. Give me a chance."

Ian reached out and casually took my hand. Much to

my chagrin, that odd sizzle of attraction shot right up my arm. But it was a lot weaker than it had been last week. Possibly because the guy was turning out to be a complete egomaniac who couldn't take a hint.

I pulled my hand away and wiped it on my jeans for effect, as if his touch had skeeved me out.

"Sorry, Ian," I said, backing away. "I'm with Nate. Get used to it."

Then I got out of there as fast as I possibly could.

"Omigod. What a loser," Cara said as we shared a plate of fries at Johnny's after school. Both of our boyfriends had after-school commitments, so we were killing time waiting for them—a first for us. "Doesn't he realize how pathetic he is? He practically threw himself at you."

"Well, who could blame him?" I joked, as I dipped a fry into a ketchup-mustard mix. "But seriously, Cara. The whole time I was petrified that Nate would come around the corner and see us and think that all the rumors about me were true."

"He wouldn't think that," Cara said.

"Why not? He has to be a little bit paranoid after reading all that crap on the Daze. A little visual confirmation might be all he'd need." I felt ill just thinking about it and pushed my fries away. Why had I ever volunteered to help Ian? If only I had never raised my hand that day in class, I wouldn't have to deal with this now.

"Layla, you didn't do anything wrong," Cara pointed out. "You were just telling Mr. Can't Take No For An Answer to back off. It's completely fine."

"I hope you're right," I said.

Cara took a sip of her soda, staring me down. "What is it, Layla? Why are you so paranoid?"

Because before I decided for sure Nate was the one for me, I did cheat on him. Twice—with Drew. Because I thought about cheating on him with Ian. And because I'm so, so scared he's going to find out and hate me.

"I don't know," I said, squirming. "Nate and I are having such a good time I guess I'm just . . . waiting for something bad to happen."

Cara gave me a sympathetic look. "Don't let Ian do this to you," she said. "You and Nate are a great couple. Nothing bad is going to happen."

"Promise?" I asked hopefully.

Cara grinned confidently. "Promise."

I only wished I felt as sure as she did.

When Nate and I got back to my house we found a note from my mom in the kitchen. She was out buying supplies and would be back in two hours.

"Well, what're we gonna do until then?" Nate asked flirtatiously.

I smiled and took his hand. "I have a few ideas."

I led Nate to my room, jumped onto my bed, and leaned against the headboard. Nate went straight for my CDs to find something good to listen to.

"I'm telling you, I haven't bought any new CDs in forever," I said. "Everything good is on my iPod."

Nate gave me a sidelong grin. "If by 'good' you mean Jessica Simpson, then all I have to say is 'whatever,'" he teased.

I grabbed a pillow and chucked it at him. He ducked, and I giggled. "And I suppose those Aaron Carter songs you've got on your iPod are better, huh?" I mocked him in return. "And don't try to tell me you downloaded them for your little sister."

"I did!" Nate said, laughing. He went into his backpack and pulled out a homemade CD. "It doesn't matter, anyway. I've got the perfect mood music."

A slow, jazzy R & B tune flowed from the speakers of my CD player. "Nice," I said. "You always carry that around with you just hoping to get lucky?"

"Yeah. I'm a player," Nate joked. "Actually, it's a mix my dad made to try to get me into his music."

"And you're using it as makeout music?" I said as he crawled onto my bed. "How would dear old dad feel about that?"

"I have an idea. How about we don't talk about my father anymore?" Nate said, pulling me toward him.

"Good plan."

Without another word, he kissed me. As I wrapped my arms around him, Nate ran his hand under my shirt and over the bare skin of my stomach. I felt a twinge of tenderness and suddenly Nate sat up.

"Whoa." He lifted my shirt and stared at my navel ring. "That wasn't here before."

Oh, God. Think fast!

"Right," I said, pushing myself up a bit.

"When did you get that?" Nate asked.

Okay. This was not good. What was I supposed to say? *Remember that day I didn't return your calls? Well, I was really out with Drew Sullivan getting our bodies defaced together. Oh, and he totally kissed me.*

"That? I got it . . . uh. . . ."

Not fast enough, Layla.

Nate was clearly starting to get suspicious.

"What's up?" he asked, moving away from me slightly.

All right, it was time to start lying. It was time to start lying my ass off. So much for that trust thing. The best I could do was try to work in a teeny bit of truth.

"Well, the other day, Cara and I went shopping, and we ran into Drew Sullivan." I swallowed hard, just hoping I didn't look *too* guilty. "Anyway, he said he was doing some work at Vinny's Tattoo Palace."

"So you guys spontaneously decided to get your belly buttons pierced? Why does that not sound like something Cara Matz would be up for?" Nate said.

"I was just as surprised as you when Cara suggested we do it, believe me."

Believe me? Yeah, right.

"But then, of course, she made me go first and as soon as she saw how painful it was, she totally chickened out."

Was that any better? I couldn't tell if he was buying it or not.

"So, why didn't you tell me?" he asked, sounding a little hurt. "I mean, you knew I'd see it at some point."

Yeah, I hadn't thought of that. I had been too caught up with impressing Drew.

"I'm sorry," I said. "I didn't think it was that big a deal."

Nate took a breath. "It's okay," he said. Then he smiled devilishly. "Actually, it's really hot."

I gulped. Unfortunately that reminded me of Drew's reaction to the piercing. The one he'd had right before he kissed me.

"Really?" I squeaked.

"Mmmhmm."

He leaned in to kiss me and my breath caught. For the first time his kiss wasn't just sweet and yummy, but passionate. I was so pleasantly surprised that I giggled as he rolled on top of me.

"You're so beautiful, Layla," he said, pulling away and looking me in the eye.

My heart thumped extra hard. "You are, too," I said.

Then he kissed me again and I hoped that would be the end of Ian Cramer and Drew Sullivan or any other guy.

I didn't want to lie or even *think* about my secrets ever again. I wanted to concentrate on Nate alone.

fourteen

Tuesday afternoon during eighth period, one of the office assistants dropped by my Chem class and handed Mr. Roswell a pink pass. Everyone in the room froze. We all knew what a pink pass meant. Someone was being summoned to the vice principal's office, which was never good.

"Miss Carter?"

My heart dropped. In the back of the room, Debra Jack snickered.

"Gather your things," Mr. Roswell said. "Mr. Harris would like to see you."

I quickly got up and grabbed my bag and books. Everyone stared as I walked out with the office assistant.

"Can you get expelled for sleeping around?" someone stage whispered, earning a few laughs.

It was all I could do to keep from flipping the bird at the whole room on my way out.

"Mr. Harris? I have Layla Carter for you," the assistant said when we reached the open door of his office.

"Layla, thank you for coming in," Mr. Harris said somberly. His stomach rolls adjusted as he sat down in his large, leather chair. "Have a seat." He gestured to a chair opposite his desk.

The office assistant closed the door behind me. I tried not to feel nervous. After all, as far as I knew I hadn't done anything wrong—lately. But Mr. Harris's office—with its lack of windows and austere message posters about doing the right thing—was always an intimidating place.

"Thanks," I said lightly, tucking my skirt under me as I sat. I placed my books and bag on the floor next to the chair and cleared my throat. Mr. Harris looked me over, lacing his fingers together on hid desk.

"Layla, I need to speak with you about this Kensington Daze website that *The Reporter* is running," he began.

I inhaled sharply at the mention of the Daze. Don't tell me Mr. Harris had been reading it too. Oh, God. *Please* don't let him have seen the street-walker thing.

"Many members of the faculty, myself included, have read this forum, and we're very concerned," Mr. Harris said dryly.

Come on! I said *don't* tell me Mr. Harris has been reading it. Wasn't anyone listening out there?

"I'm sure you've read it yourself, so you, better than

anyone, can understand our concern," he continued.

I had to get out of here. Like, now.

"So I wanted to find out from you where the staff stands on keeping Kensington Daze running," he finished finally.

I looked into Mr. Harris's tired, yet hopeful, eyes. I could tell he wanted me to tell him we were taking it down. He had probably called me in here, instead of Cara, because he had seen what the rumor-posters were doing to me. He probably thought I wanted the thing killed even more than he did. But I had to be pragmatic about this.

"Well, Mr. Harris, *The Reporter* staff knows the Daze is problematic, but it's been incredible for ad sales and readership," I explained. "To be honest, we've been struggling with the decision of whether to shut it down or not."

Mr. Harris narrowed his eyes at me. This look of his was infamous. And if it was followed by a sigh, you knew the next thing he said was going to be harsh.

He sighed.

"Well, I must say the administrators here are experiencing no such struggle," he told me. "I was hoping you would have already come to the same conclusions we had, but it seems I'm going to have to make the decision for you and your staff. I want the site down by the end of the week."

I felt a *whoosh* rush through me. It felt a lot like relief. But I also knew that no one on the staff was going to like being unilaterally told what to do. Not even Cara.

"But, sir . . ." I said weakly.

"I'm sorry, Miss Carter," he said, shuffling some papers around. "That site will accomplish nothing positive for this school. Take it down or suffer the consequences."

Well. There was no arguing with that. "Okay," I said, standing. "I'll . . . tell the staff."

"Thank you for your time," Mr. Harris said.

I turned and slipped out. Once my heart stopped pounding, I found myself smiling. It was over. Debra Jack would no longer have a forum for ripping me to shreds. It was actually over.

After the last bell, I headed for my locker to grab my books and wait for Nate. I hummed to myself as I worked my lock. This had turned out to be a pretty good day.

"What's up, Lay-la-la?"

Great. Way to jinx myself.

"Not much," I said coolly, glancing at Ian out of the corner of my eye. Every day it was getting easier and easier to control that flirt reflex.

"When are you going to drop the act and go out with me already?" Ian said mischievously, leaning back against the row of lockers.

Was he kidding me? "Ian, listen, I don't mean to be blunt, but take the hint already," I said, shoving my heavy Chem text into my locker with a bang. "I'm not going to go out with you."

Slowly, Ian smiled. "Come on, Layla. I know you want me."

I laughed. "Oh, my God. Do you even hear yourself?

Where, exactly, does that ego of yours come from?"

Ian shrugged. "It's not ego. I just figure if you're going to give it up to everyone else, why not me?"

I felt as if someone had just tipped the floor beneath me and I gripped my locker door. For a split second I was actually afraid I might faint. That's what this was all about? The stupid website? He just wanted to get lucky?

Ian leaned in so close to my ear his dreadlocks grazed my shoulder. "Come on, Layla. You won't be disappointed. You've been with tons of boys. Maybe it's time to try a man."

I couldn't believe he was saying these things to me. I tried to take in a deep breath, but it got caught in my throat. Ian ran his finger down my arm.

"I'll make it worth your time," he whispered.

Okay. Enough was enough. I opened my mouth to tell him exactly what he could do with the stupid Kensington Daze.

"Layla?"

My eyes widened.

Ian smirked.

We both looked up to find Nate standing three feet away from us, stunned and pale.

Instantly I realized what this looked like. Ian had been standing close enough for our cheeks to be touching. He was touching my arm and his dreads had fallen forward to hide our faces. For all Nate knew, we could have been kissing.

"Hello, mate," Ian said.

Nate glared at him for a second, then looked at me. His ears were gradually turning bright red.

"What's going on, Layla?" he demanded.

"Not what you think," I said, finding my voice. My heart was having a panic attack of unprecedented proportions.

"Or it might be *exactly* what you think," Ian said, raising his eyebrows.

"What is your problem?!" I shouted at Ian.

"I'm outta here," Nate said. With one ice-cold look at me, he turned and stormed away.

"You, never talk to me again," I said to Ian. He grinned and backed up, hands raised. I turned and ran after my boyfriend. "Nate! Wait up!"

Nate stopped and turned to face me. The chill in his eyes nearly knocked the wind right out of me.

"What the hell *was* that?" he yelled, throwing a hand up in the air.

"Ian keeps asking me out and I keep saying no, but—"

"I thought you said you guys were just friends," Nate spat back.

"I did. I mean, we were," I said. "I mean, I thought we were—"

Dammit. Why couldn't I get my thoughts straight? This wasn't helping.

"Well, clearly he had some reason to think otherwise," Nate said, turning around again. He headed for the lobby at mach 10.

"Wait a minute!" I said, rushing after him. "What's that supposed to mean?"

"It means what it means, Layla," Nate said, his hand on the door handle. He was so ready to bolt he could have been a skittish race horse.

"Hold up. So you're saying you think I was leading him on?" I said, my face hot with anger. "You think I *wanted* him to practically grope me like that in the middle of the hallway?"

"I don't know, maybe," Nate said. He looked at me and sighed. There was so much anger and hurt and confusion in his expression it was practically radiating off of him. "I don't know what to think right now."

Then it hit me like a fist to the gut.

"Oh, my God. You believe the rumors, don't you?" I said, backing up slightly. "You think it's all true. What was all that crap about trusting me? About just the two of us?"

"That was before I saw you all over *him*," Nate said. "I gotta go, Layla."

"Wait a minute," I said, stopping him in his tracks. My heart was in my throat, but there was no way I was letting him off the hook that easy. "What are we saying here?" I asked.

"What do you mean?" he blurted.

"Look, I know that I only want to be with you," I said tremulously. "I know where *I* stand. But if you can't trust me, then this is as good as over."

I stared at him, my heart on my sleeve, just hoping he wouldn't tear it off and stomp on it. He had no idea how unprecedented this was. I had never let myself be this vulnerable before. Not once.

Nate looked me in the eye. "Then I guess it's over."

And just like that, he was gone.

fifteen

Not only was Nate not waiting for me by my locker on Wednesday morning, which was bad enough, but Debra, Hannah, and Erica *were*. I knew word of my public breakup with Nate was making its way through the airwaves. They were whispering when I arrived, but as soon as they spotted me, they shushed themselves and watched my approach like hawks hovering before the kill. I took a deep breath and walked over, my head held high. I had never let these losers see me run before. No reason to start now.

"Good morning, Layla!" Debra said cheerily. "You're looking a little pale this morning. Is everything okay?"

"Get a life, Debra," I said, opening my locker.

Debra hit me with a wry smile. Nothing was getting her down today. She was victorious and we all knew it.

"I'm really sorry about you and Nate, sweetie," she said, rubbing my arm cruelly. "But it had to happen sooner or later. You just weren't meant for each other."

I snatched my arm away. "Look, Debra, you've done your job, okay? Your incessant blogging worked. Why don't you just go party already? Get something waxed in celebration."

Erica snorted a laugh and Debra shot her a look of death. "Don't shoot the messenger," Debra said. "It's not like I wrote anything on that site that everyone didn't already know."

I slammed my locker and she jumped. "You got what you wanted. Don't ever talk to me as if we both don't know that you made all the crap up. It's insulting. To both of us."

"Touchy touchy," Debra said. Then she looked at her friends. "Come on, you guys, let's find Nate. I'm sure he needs a little comforting."

They walked off and I shook my head. "Who's the slut now?" I said under my breath. Frustrated, I kicked my locker and a couple of people shot me disturbed looks.

"Everything okay?"

I turned around to find Cara hovering behind me.

"Not exactly," I said. "I could just kill that girl."

Cara looped her arm around mine. "I understand the compulsion," she said. "But unfortunately, if you do that, they're gonna send you away for the rest of your life and that is just not an option. I'd never make it through the rest of the year without you."

I forced a smile and tried to perk up, but it was impossible. Nate was in this school somewhere and it was just a matter of time before we bumped into each other. I dreaded it with every fiber of my being.

"Listen," Cara said. "We don't have any tests today. Why don't we just cut and go do something fun?"

"Like what?" I said grumpily.

"Shop?" she suggested. "We can drive to the mall."

Shopping didn't appeal to me, but I had a feeling nothing would just then. The idea of getting out of school, however, was definitely appetizing.

"Fine," I said. "Let's go."

I turned around and walked right into Darren Rourke and his girlfriend Missy Tyler.

"Watch where you're going," Missy chirped.

"Sorry," I mumbled.

As they walked away I heard Missy say to Darren, "Did you hear? Nate finally dumped her."

"Guess *Most Likely to Give It Up* finally gave it up," Darren said with a laugh.

I narrowed my eyes, my face flushing with heat. Suddenly I knew exactly what I wanted to do with my day.

"Screw the mall," I told Cara. "I have a better idea."

Five minutes later Cara and I were locked in the *Reporter* office and Cara was taping black construction paper over the window in the door.

"Gee. This is fun," she said.

"I know you'd rather be trying on clothes, but I have to do this, and the blog is only going to be up for two more days," I said, booting up my computer.

"Okay, what can I do?" Cara said.

I brought up the *Hall of Shame*. "Do you think you can copy the design?" I said.

"Sure," Cara replied with a shrug. "Mike taught me a thing or two," she said, sitting down at the computer next to mine. "What do you want to call it?"

"How about *Layla Carter's Personal Hall of Shame*?" I suggested, feeling a thrill of excitement.

Cara nodded. "I'm on it."

"Good. Now all I have to do is figure out what I want to say. . . . "

A few hours later and it was done. Cara's banner was perfect and under it was my message to the students of Kensington High.

To Whom It May Concern:

I know you have been reading a lot of things about me on this blog recently, and let me be the first to say how proud I am of all of you. It's so heartening to learn that you are so eager to believe everything that you read. If the people of our generation are this gullible, I weep for our future. This country is in serious trouble.

Now, I'm not going to sit here and try to refute every single lie that each of you has posted on this site, because 1) I have better things to do with my time 2) I don't really care what you people think of me, and 3) You probably wouldn't believe it anyway. I know it's much more attractive to believe the scandal.

But what I will say is how very ashamed I am to have counted so many of you as my friends over the years. Some of you didn't try very hard to disguise who you were (nice stabs at anonymous screen names, guys). Thanks to the details of your stories (the details that *were* true) I know exactly who is telling which lies. So to anyone who posted complete lies, I have one message: I hope you're proud of yourselves. I hope you're proud of the fact that you've completely obliterated some very sweet memories I may have had of you. I hope you can still look at yourselves in the mirror. But most of all I hope that one day you realize how truly horrible you've been and that once you realize it, you'll make sure never to be that horrible again. Because some of you are, at heart, nice guys, and unless you figure out how to be those guys again, no girl out there is ever going to want you.

Well, that's it. Thanks for the past few weeks, people. It's been good times. Can't wait to party with you on senior weekend and at prom. I'm sure it'll be a blast.

Sincerely,
Layla Carter

P.S. Thanks to your total lack of morals and decorum, the administration has decided to kill this site as of Friday. Hope you all had fun while it lasted.

"Wow, Layla. That's amazing," Cara said, once she was finished reading over my shoulder.

"I like it," I said with a proud smile. "Taking the high road feels good."

The bell rang and we glanced at the clock. It was already fifth period. Time for lunch.

"Johnny's?" Cara suggested with a shrug.

I slapped my notebook closed and shut the computer down, feeling much lighter than I had that morning. Light enough, even, to face the huge crowd of my classmates that would be gathered at Johnny's. "Sounds like a plan."

When Cara and I reached the parking lot, we stopped in our tracks. A huge crowd had gathered on the other side of the student section and a bunch of them were yelling and cheering.

"What the—"

"Fight!" some guy shouted, tearing by us toward the crowd.

Cara and I glanced at one another and ran over. Fights weren't all that common at our school and my curiosity surged as we tried to push our way to the front of the crowd.

A bunch of people gasped and jumped back. I saw an arm hit the asphalt and a few people parted to make room. Suddenly the two guys were right there at my feet, whaling on each other.

And one of them was Nate Henry.

"Nate! What are you doing?" I shouted.

He didn't even look up. Didn't seem to hear me. He slammed his fist into Kyle Larame's face over and over again. Kyle writhed under him, raising his hands to try to block the blows.

"Get off me, man!" he shouted.

"Nate! Stop!" I said, near tears. It was like he was possessed. I never would have imagined he could be so angry.

"Out of the way! Out of the way!"

Mr. Harris came barreling through the crowd along with Coach Krantz. Coach grabbed Nate around the shoulders and yanked him right off Kyle. Nate's lip was cut and blood poured from his nose, but he still struggled against Coach's grip. Mr. Harris helped Kyle off the ground.

"What's your problem, man?" he shouted at Nate. "You know it's true!"

"Shut your mouth, or I'll do it for you!" Nate came back at him with a ferocious rage. What had Kyle said to Nate to make him go so ballistic? And why did I have a sinking feeling that it had something to do with me?

"That's enough! Both of you, into my office! Now!" Mr. Harris shouted.

As Nate followed the vice principal and the coach into the school, our eyes met. I tried to let him know telepathically how worried I was about him, but he just stared back at me. Then he turned and followed Mr. Harris inside.

That night I was sitting on my bed listening to my iPod and holding my cell phone, trying to decide whether or not to call Nate, when my mother stuck her head into my room.

"Hi, honey. I got you something," she said.

She slipped into my room and handed me a brand-new

bag of Double Stuf Oreos and a glass of milk. My absolute favorite cookie. I had only been officially allowed to have them twice in my life. Once in sixth grade when I had broken my leg falling off my bike, and then again a couple years ago—the day my dad had left. Mom had even eaten a few that day.

"Wow. You must be really worried about me," I said. I'd told her about everything earlier that afternoon.

"Well, the milk's still soy," my mom said apologetically. "But go crazy with the cookies. You deserve a break."

"Thanks, Mom," I said, forcing a smile.

"I love you, sweet cheeks," she said, leaning down to kiss the top of my head.

"Love you, too."

My cell phone rang when she was on her way out the door. She paused and looked at me, eyebrows raised, and my heart fluttered with hope. Could it be?

I checked the caller ID and the flutter died.

"It's just Cara," I said.

My mother smiled. "Tell her I said, 'hi.'" Then she closed the door behind her.

"Hey, Cara," I said, picking up the call. I set the cookies and milk aside.

"You're not going to believe what Mike just told me," she began. "Guess what caused the fight today between Nate and Kyle."

"I'm not sure I want to know," I admitted, "but tell me anyway."

"Okay, Kyle made some crack about you to Nate, and—"

"What did Kyle say?" I broke in.

Cara hesitated. "Well . . ."

"Just say it fast," I told her, pretty much knowing what was coming. "It's less painful that way."

"Well, he was giving Nate props for dumping you because he thinks you're . . . a slut."

Ouch.

"So Nate decked him," Cara added. "And now he's suspended for the rest of the week for fighting on school grounds."

I couldn't believe it. Nate, the BMOC, had gotten suspended. For me.

"So Nate was kind of . . . defending me?" I asked with a smile.

"Duh!" Cara cried impatiently. "He *so* still likes you."

"Maybe," I said, trying not to hope. "But Cara, he said some awful things to me. Maybe I don't still like him."

"Oh, please. We both know you do," Cara said. "Look, maybe he wants to apologize, but is just chickening out. You don't know. Maybe you should give him the chance."

"So what do I do now?" I asked her, my heart thumping extra hard. "Should I call him? Go over there? What?"

"Bare minimum? Call him," Cara agreed. "Do it now before you lose your nerve."

"I don't know—"

"Do it!" Cara repeated. "And then call me back."

The line went dead and I stared at my phone for a moment. Then I took a deep breath and tore open the bag of Oreos. I was going to need some sugar strength for this one. I took a bite, then dialed.

As the phone rang I swallowed, then held my breath. When the line picked up I nearly had a heart attack, but it was just his voicemail.

"Hey. This is Nate. Leaving a message would be great . . . crap, I rhymed. How do I erase—*BEEEEP*."

I smiled upon hearing the familiar message, then remembered I was supposed to be talking now. Oops.

"Nate, it's Layla," I began. "I heard about what happened with Kyle. I just wanted to say thanks. And maybe we could, I don't know, talk? Anyway, call me when you get this. Okay, bye."

I hung up the phone and groaned. Way to be awkward. I hit Cara's speed-dial button.

"Well?" she said.

"He didn't pick up. Do you think he's screening?" I said.

"I don't know. Maybe he doesn't feel like talking to anyone right now," she said. "Keep trying."

"But I just left a message," I said.

"Keep trying anyway," she recommended. "Send him an e-mail, too. You guys have to talk this out."

"Okay. Thanks, Cara."

"Anytime. Call me if you need me."

I hung up the phone and grabbed another Oreo before heading for my computer. Cara was right. I had done a few things that I regretted and it was quite possible that Nate had said a few things that he regretted. Maybe if we could just get it all out in the open, we could, I don't know, fix things between us somehow.

The only thing I knew for certain was that I missed him. That I wanted him back. I had felt what it was like to have the perfect boyfriend and if there was a chance I could have that again, I would fight for it.

I just hoped Nate wanted to fight for it, too.

sixteen

Saturday morning I drove my mother's car right over to Nate's house. Two days had passed. Two full days with no word from him. He hadn't answered my calls or my e-mails and I couldn't take it anymore. I had to talk to him—even if he told me to just leave him alone. I had to know for sure how he felt.

My knees quaked as I climbed out of the car in front of his house.

Okay, it's going to be fine, I told myself, wiping my sweaty palms on my jeans. *Just get it over with.*

I reached out and rang the bell. No one answered. For almost three minutes I was in total agony, wondering whether to ring again or just retreat. Then I heard a click and his mother opened the door.

"Oh, hello, Layla," she said. "What brings you here?"

"Hi, Mrs. Henry. I was hoping to talk to Nate," I said, holding my breath. "Is he home?"

"I'm sorry, hon, but Nate is grounded for the rest of the weekend," she said. "I'll tell him you came by."

Total devastation. "Oh. Okay. Thanks."

She smiled apologetically and closed the door. Slowly, I turned around and started back down the front walk. I couldn't believe that was it. I had spent half the morning psyching myself up to drive over here and that was all I got?

I paused halfway down the walk and looked back at the house. If Nate was grounded he was in there somewhere. And Layla Carter did not give up that easily.

Quickly, I ducked around the side of the house and made my way along the garage. I checked around the corner into the backyard and it was deserted. No sign of Nate's dad or his little sister. I took a deep breath and glanced up at Nate's bedroom. Something flashed by the window. He was in there! Now all I had to do was figure out how to get to him.

I pulled my cell phone out and dialed Nate's number. Once again, it went directly to voicemail.

"Damn," I said under my breath. What was I supposed to do now?

A cool wind tossed my hair around my face and rustled the branches of the tree next to me. They scratched at Nate's window up above.

They *scratched* at Nate's *window*.

I smiled mischievously. Suddenly I knew exactly what I had to do. I reached out and grabbed the lowest branch. The thick oak was perfect for climbing, as if it had been put there for this very reason. It had been a long time since I'd scaled a tree, but with little effort, I reached a large limb that stretched out above the back porch roof. I swung down, placed my feet on the roof's surface, and grinned. Too easy.

I walked right over to Nate's window and knocked. He appeared at the pane two seconds later, looking utterly scared and totally gorgeous.

Oh, crap. I had been so intent on my "Mission: Impossible" I had completely spaced on the fact that I had to talk to him now.

Nate pushed open his window and leaned out. "Layla! what the hell are you doing?" he whispered.

"I . . . uh, needed to talk to you," I said, biting my lip.

"If my parents catch you out there, they're gonna kill us both," he said.

"So, invite me in?" I suggested.

Nate sighed, but clearly could think of no other option. He backed up so I could crawl through the window.

"What's up?" he whispered, standing in the middle of his room.

"Didn't you get any of my messages?" I asked. "My e-mails?" If he had, we would have already known what was up.

"I'm grounded. No phone, no computer 'til Monday."

"Oh. Right." Duh, Layla. "Well, I heard what you and

Kyle were fighting about and I just wanted to say thanks," I told him. "After the stuff you said to me on Tuesday I didn't really think you'd be defending my honor."

Nate looked at the floor. "Yeah, about that," he said. "I'm really sorry I freaked out. It was just, when I saw you with that guy—"

"I know," I said. "I actually understand."

"You do?" he said hopefully.

"Sort of. I mean, it couldn't have looked good," I said. Then I took a deep breath and shoved my hands into the back pockets of my jeans. I had to do this. There was no way around it. If Nate and I were ever going to have a chance he had to know the truth. "And to be honest, your suspicions weren't *totally* unfounded."

"Oh boy," Nate said, sitting down on the end of his bed. "Do I want to hear this?"

"I'm not sure, but I'm going to tell you," I said. "When we first started dating I was sort of still . . . dating around," I said, trying to put it as delicately as possible. "Not with Ian. With Drew Sullivan."

Nate looked ill.

"I had a feeling there was something weird about that belly button piercing story," he said.

Guess I wasn't as good a liar as I thought. Was that a good thing or a bad thing?

"I don't know if this is a defense or not, but we had never said we were exclusive and I just . . . that's what I've always done," I said, my heart slamming around in my rib cage. "Dated around."

"Okay," Nate said slowly.

"But Nate, I don't want to do that anymore," I said, sitting down next to him on the bed. "I only want to be with you."

Nate turned and studied my eyes. "How do I believe you?" he said. "How do I know you're telling the truth?"

I lifted my shoulders. "I guess you just have to decide whether or not *you* want to be with *me*," I said. "And if you do, then you just have to . . . take a leap of faith."

I reached out and took his hand. The fact that he didn't pull away had to be a good sign.

"And then there's this," I said.

I leaned in, ever so slowly, and kissed him. My pulse raced in my ears and my entire body sizzled. Finally, slowly, Nate slipped his hands over my thighs and around my waist. I smiled as I deepened the kiss.

He was kissing me back! He was kissing me back!

"Whoa," Nate said when I pulled away.

I smiled, breathless. "I don't know about you, but I like the way that feels," I said. "No one else has *ever* made me feel that way."

Nate took a deep breath and pulled me into the crook of his arm. I cuddled into him, relief washing through me.

"So, a leap of faith, huh?" he said.

"Yeah," I replied hopefully.

"I think I could be up for that," he said.

"Really?" I sat up straight and looked into his perfect blue eyes.

"I missed you, Layla," he said.

A pleasant warmth rushed all through me. No one had ever said that to me before.

"I missed you, too," I told him.

Then he touched his lips to mine and I knew. Just like I knew that everything was going to be all right. I was kissing my boyfriend. My very first boyfriend. And I was happy.

The End

The Choice Redux

So, how did I do? Was Nate the right choice, or do you think someone else would be more exciting? If this ending wasn't good enough for you, turn back to page 103 and try again.

You Chose Ian

twelve

"That's it. I know what I have to do," I said.

"I knew it! You're coming to the dance, right?" Cara said with a grin.

"Uh, no. I'm going to the Bloodworms concert," I said, grabbing my phone.

"Really?" Cara said, leaning into the counter. "But you hardly even know Ian."

"I know, but that's part of the intrigue," I said. "Come on, Cara. He is *so* hot. And I really like Nate, but if I keep dating him you know I'm gonna get bored eventually. He's, like, Mr. High School. Ian is—"

"Going to take you into the city to hang out with our favorite band of all time," Cara said with a sigh. "I know. It does seem pretty darn obvious when you put it that way."

"I was going to say Ian is exotic, well-traveled, and interesting, but yeah. There is the added bonus of the fact that he personally knows Necro Phillips," I said.

"Okay, well, have a good time," Cara said, reaching out for a hug. "I hate you, you know that."

"I'll get them to sign something for you," I promised.

"You'd better. I guess I'll go pick up Mike for the dance," she said, fluttering her fingers. "Good luck with your phone calls."

My stomach clenched and I looked down at the phone in my hand. "Yeah. Thanks."

This was not going to be fun.

"Layla! Hey! How are you feeling?" Nate said the moment he picked up the phone. "Are you going to be okay for the dance?"

Crap. Could he make this any harder? Why did he have to be so sweet? I sat down on the end of my bed and gripped the comforter with my free hand.

"Actually, I'm feeling better. Thanks for asking," I said. "But, about the dance—"

"What's up?" Nate asked, totally clueless that anything bad was coming.

"God, Nate, I hate to do this to you, but I'm not gonna make it tonight," I said, wincing.

"What? Why?" he asked.

"It's just, all this talk of anniversaries and Valentine's Day," I said, getting up to pace the floor. "I feel like we're going too fast."

"Oh."

There had never been so much disappointment in one word before. Never.

"I'm sorry, Nate. I really like you, but I have some stuff I need to figure out before I can be in a serious relationship," I said.

"Right. Well. Okay, then," he said. "I guess I should just . . ."

"I'm really sorry, Nate," I said again.

"Yeah, well, me, too I guess," Nate said, thoroughly confused. "I'll see ya, Layla."

"Okay. Well, bye."

I hung up the phone and took a deep breath. Just like that, I was officially single again. Quickly I dialed Drew's number, now very eager to get this over with. The first thing I heard when he picked up the line was the wail of an electric guitar.

"Hello?" he shouted.

"Drew!? It's Layla!" I shouted back.

"Oh. Hey, Layla," he said.

I heard a trill of female laughter in the background and Drew chuckled as well. My whole body instantly overheated.

"What're you doing?" I asked.

"Getting ready for the show," he said. "Got some friends over."

Yeah. Female friends.

"I'll be right there, babe," he said, holding the phone away.

Babe? *Babe?* Who was he talking to? Unbelievable. One day he's kissing me and inviting me to see his work and the next he's calling other girls *babe*? What was *with* this guy? Apparently I had made the right decision here.

"Drew! Hey, Drew!" I said.

"Sorry. Yeah?" he said, returning his attention to the phone.

"Listen, I'm not gonna make it tonight," I said. "I got tickets to this concert and I'm going to that instead."

"Oh. Well. That sucks," he said.

"Does it?" I said shrilly as another round of laughter sounded in the background.

"What?" he shouted.

"Nothing," I told him. "Good-bye."

I hung up the phone, tossed it on my bed, and grabbed my jeans. Suddenly I couldn't wait to see Ian.

thirteen

"So Necro is absolutely blasted and he backs into Jake's massive tank of boa constrictors," Ian said, laughing as he told his story.

"Wait a minute, boa constrictors?" I said, stopping him with a hand on his arm. A half dozen other concert-goers scooted around us, heading down the street toward the entrance to the theater.

"Yeah. Jake takes them everywhere," Ian said. "So Necro backs into them and the whole tank shatters, and Donnie had left the door to the suite open—"

"No!" I said.

"Yes! And those buggers are *quick*."

"Oh, do not tell me. They got out into the hotel?" I said with a laugh.

"You guessed it. We spent the entire night hunting those things down. The entire place was bedlam. Ladies screaming, people calling the police," he said. "Wild times."

"Wow. Your life is insane," I said. Ian had been telling stories ever since we'd gotten on the train back in Kensington. I would have killed to have had half the cool experiences he'd had.

"I suppose you could say that, yeah," Ian said with a smile.

I took a deep breath of the cool, city air and smiled. New York was hopping, as always—a cacophony of horn honks, shouted greetings, and random music spilling from apartment windows and cars. Everywhere I looked couples were huddled together on their way to romantic dinners, or packs of people were making their way down the street to theaters and parties. I loved coming into New York City. Whenever I was there I felt like something amazing was going to happen.

"Well, shall we?" Ian asked, taking my hand.

My entire body sizzled with anticipation as we headed toward the crowd thronging outside the theater. Ian led me right past the huge SOLD OUT! sign and over to the alley on the side of the building.

"This is a much better way," he said when we came to a green metal door.

"Oh, right. We're 'with the band,'" I said excitedly. Then I got a good look at the entrance. "Uh, Ian? There's no handle on this door."

"Oh, ye of little faith," he said.

He gave the door three hard bangs, followed by four quick beats. Instantly the door opened and a huge bouncer in a black T-shirt grinned at us.

"Ian, my brother!" he shouted.

"Hey, man!" Ian greeted him with a quick but elaborate handshake. "This is Layla."

"Hi," I said.

"Hi," the bouncer replied, looking me over appreciatively. "Wow, Ian. A few weeks in the country and already you've got yourself a gorgeous girl."

"Thanks," I said, blushing.

"Hands off. She's mine," Ian said, pulling me past him.

I laughed as we slipped down a hallway lined with stage lights and random wiring. Already the opening band, the Throng, was warming up out on the stage and the music was loud enough to drown out any and all other sounds. We passed by a few closed dressing room doors and came out into one of the wings of the stage. Somewhere in this backstage area were the members of the Bloodworms. Every second I expected to stumble upon one of them. What would I say? Could I even hope to not get all gushy and stupid in front of them?

"Check it out!" Ian shouted, pausing at the edge of a black curtain. "Can't get a better view than that."

I stepped up next to him. Crosby Marx, the lead singer of the Throng, was just a few yards away and I had a perfect side view of the drum set and the ridiculously elaborate light and speaker setup.

"This is awesome!" I said. "Thank you so much for

159

bringing me here!"

"Thanks for coming along," Ian replied.

"Ian!"

"Oh, hey, Dad!" Ian said.

Ian's father was even taller than Ian with dark skin and a shaved head. He wore a black shirt and jeans and had a wireless phone attached to his ear. They hugged quickly and then Ian turned to me.

"Dad, this is Layla," he said. "Layla, my dad."

"A pleasure to meet you, Layla," Ian's father said, shaking my hand. "Mind if I steal my boy for a sec?"

"No. Go ahead," I replied.

Ian's father took him aside and they powwowed for a few minutes. The whole time I looked around my immediate area at all the bustling tech guys and grips and random workers, trying to spot a Bloodworm while trying to look as if I wasn't trying to spot a Bloodworm.

Hard work. And I saw no one.

"Sorry about that. Business," Ian said when he rejoined me. "When the concert is over, Dad wants me to go on ahead and make sure everything is okay for the after-party."

"So we're gonna be in Necro's apartment alone?" I said. "That is so cool!"

Ian laughed. "I'm glad you're here with me instead of Alexandra," he said.

"Alexandra?"

"My ex," he explained. "She's so affected that she'd probably be bored right now. But you . . . you're loving every minute of this, aren't you?"

"You have no idea," I replied.

"Good," he said, taking my hand again. "Now come on. I know exactly where we'll need to be if we want to get in on that power circle."

After an hour of deafening subpar music by the Throng, it was almost time for the Bloodworms to go on. I could practically feel the heightened adrenaline in the air as Ian and I hovered by the craft services table, absently munching on crackers and cheese.

"When are they coming out?" I asked.

"Any second now," Ian assured me.

"All right, everyone! Let's get together!" Ian's father shouted, appearing from the hallway where the dressing rooms were located. He clapped his hands together and all the workers and groupies in sight started to gather. "Necro's looking for a very powerful circle tonight for the band's first show in New York, so let's see if we can oblige, right?"

Everyone cheered. My heart started thumping in my ears. Sweat prickled my skin as all the little hairs on the back of my neck stood on end.

"So without any further ado, here they are! The Bloodworms!" Ian's dad announced.

And then, they were there, all five members of the band, striding out of the hallway as casual as can be as everyone around them applauded. I felt like I was about to faint. Necro Phillips was right there, shaggy, highlighted hair, dark sunglasses and all. He was so close I could have spit on him.

Not that I would have. But that's how close he was.

"Omigod," I said under my breath. "Omigod, omigod, omigod."

Ian laughed and grabbed my hand. "Come on. Let's get you in close."

Suddenly I was tripping forward toward the band, earning dirty looks from some of the trashy-looking groupies who had tried to get next to Necro. Ian practically elbowed them aside and shoved me into the center of the throng so that I was shoulder to shoulder with the singer I had worshipped my entire life.

He smelled like cigarettes and beer, but I didn't even care. Necro Phillips's skin was touching mine. His leather pants were rubbing up against my denim.

"Right," Necro said, glancing at me. "Let's get this started then."

Necro reached out and took my hand. I seriously almost peed in my pants. It was all I could do to keep from laughing out loud with unadulterated glee. I glanced over my shoulder at Ian and he shook his head at me and grinned.

"Thank you," I mouthed.

"You so owe me," he mouthed back.

Then I did laugh before returning my attention to the circle. I had to memorize every bit of this. The feeling of Necro's callused hand in mine, the faces of all the band members as they closed their eyes and meditated, the final drum crashes of the Throng's last song.

Thanks to Ian, I had a memory I was going to relive

over and over in my daydreams for the rest of my life. What was I ever going to do to repay him?

"That was the most amazing concert I have ever been to in my entire life!" I shouted over the ringing in my ears.

"You've said that twenty times already," Ian shouted back.

I laughed and the elevator door pinged. "Sorry. I'll shut up now."

"No need. I like it," Ian replied.

The door slid open and we stepped out of the private elevator and into Necro Phillips's swank apartment. The moment my high heels hit the marble floor I almost fell over in astonishment.

The apartment was mind-blowing. Everything in sight was black. From the marble floor to the leather couches to the gleaming linoleum bar to the pillows and throw rugs and walls. Anything that wasn't black was glass, like the tabletops and the bookshelves displaying dozens of awards. Oh, and the massive windows through which I could see nearly all of glittering Manhattan.

Ian laughed. "Incredible, isn't it?"

"Oh, just a little," I joked.

"Come on," Ian said, taking my hand. "I'll show you around."

The kitchen was state-of-the-art and decorated in a fifties retro style with red and blue appliances and a diner booth in place of a table. There was even an unspeakably lavish game room with a tremendous plasma TV and a purple-topped pool table.

"Funky," I said, running my hand along the top of a table shaped like a hand.

"I don't know where he gets this stuff," Ian said. He walked over to a pair of double doors and threw them open with a flourish. "And this, is Necro's bedroom."

"Whoa."

The bed took up almost the entire room. It looked like a double king and was covered with red and purple silk and a few animal print pillows. Swags of fabric hung from the ceiling and draped all around it, giving it the look of a harem room.

"I don't even want to know what goes on in here," I said, taking in the scene.

"Oh, you can probably imagine," Ian said mischievously.

He walked over to the bed and jumped backward onto it, kicking his legs up and laying back.

"How many supermodels do you think have slept here?" he said.

I walked over and stood at the end of the bed. "Oh, a thousand," I said with a smirk.

"Come try it out," Ian said, lifting himself up onto his elbows. "Then you can tell everyone you've been in Necro Phillips's bed."

I hesitated. "Why Ian Cramer, are you trying to seduce me?" I said flirtatiously.

Ian sat up and slid to the end of the bed. He took both my hands in his, kissed one, then the other. "Maybe," he said, looking up at me with those gorgeous brown eyes. "There's some champagne in the mini fridge over there. We could open a bottle and, you know, have a little fun before the guests arrive."

My heart pounded with nervous excitement. I had been dying to find out what it would be like to kiss Ian. But what exactly was he expecting here? I mean, the champagne, the massive bed. Was he looking for some sugar or the whole pie?

"I don't know," I said.

"Maybe this will convince you," Ian said.

He yanked me down onto his lap and I let out a yelp of surprise. But when his lips met mine everything else melted away. The amazing apartment, the expectations, everything. Ian was one amazing kisser.

"Wow," I said breathlessly.

"Seriously," Ian replied, his chest heaving.

"How long do we have before people start getting here?" I asked.

"At least half an hour," Ian said, kissing my cheek, then my neck, then my collarbone.

It felt so good I thought I might implode. Okay. Reality check, here. Why was I trying to resist this guy? He was gorgeous, he was fun, he had already treated me to the most incredible night of my life, which was only going to get better, and it wasn't like I was dating anyone else. Not anymore.

"Okay," I said finally. "But just so we're clear, we are *not* having sex."

Ian blinked and for a split second I thought I saw surprise in his eyes, but then he smiled.

"As long as I get another one of those kisses I'm good," he said.

"Well then," I said, getting up and walking around the massive bed. I sat down, leaned back against the pillows, and crossed my legs at the ankle. "Let's get started."

Ian laughed and crawled across the bed toward me, then sunk into me and covered his lips with mine once more. Pretty soon I forgot all about time and the guests and even the band. I was lost in Ian's touch.

Nothing else seemed real. All there was in the world was me and Ian and this crazy comfortable bed.

And it was fabulous.

fourteen

Something was ringing.

I opened my eyes and looked around me in confusion. Where the hell was I? And what was that incessant ringing?

"Are you gonna answer that?"

My heart hit my throat. Omigod. Ian. I was in bed with Ian. I had fallen asleep in Necro Phillips's bed with Ian Cramer and my cell phone was ringing.

"Oh crap," I muttered, crawling to the end of the bed. I grabbed my bag up off the floor and fumbled through it for my phone. The caller ID read HOME and the time at the top of the screen read 3:32 A.M.

I was totally dead. I didn't have a curfew, but I also hadn't called my mother to check in. This was her calling to verbally murder me.

"Hi, Mom," I said, squeezing my eyes shut.

"Layla? Where are you? Are you okay?"

"Mom, I'm so sorry," I said. "I can't believe it's three-thirty. I fell asleep at Ian's friend's place in the city. I'm such an idiot. Do you want me to come home?"

"No, don't do that," my mother replied, to my surprise. "I don't want you taking the train this late at night if you can avoid it. Are you okay there? Can you stay?"

I glanced over at Ian, who had fallen right back to sleep. "I think so," I said. "I'll call you if anything changes. Otherwise I'll see you tomorrow."

"Okay, hon," she said.

"Mom? Thanks for not being mad," I said.

"Layla, you know I trust you," she said. "Just try to remember to call next time."

We said good night and I hung up the phone and looked around. Something was definitely wrong here. Ian and I had gotten back to Necro's place four hours ago and the place was silent as a tomb. Where the hell was everybody?

"Ian?" I said, gently shaking his shoulder. "Hey, Ian. Wake up."

He snorted and lifted his head. "Whassup?"

"We fell asleep," I told him loudly. "What happened to the party?"

Ian lifted his head up farther and looked around, as if searching for the guests in the room.

"Well. That's a good question," he said. He cleared his throat and sat up, reaching for the phone on the nightstand. He dialed quickly and let out a huge yawn, flicking his dreads out of his face. Somehow, he didn't seem all that perplexed.

"Hey, Dad," he said into the phone. "Where am *I*? Where the bloody hell are you?"

I raised my eyebrows. If I talked to my mom that way she would have keeled over.

"What? You're joking," he glanced at me and rolled his eyes. "Oh, bollocks. Yeah, yeah. Sorry. Yeah. All right. See you, then." He hung up the phone and turned to me. "Well, I'm an idiot."

"What happened?" I asked.

"The party was at Rodrigo's place downstairs. It's all but petered out now."

"Rodrigo? The keyboard player?"

"Yeah. His apartment is one floor below this one. I have both sets of keys. I just got the instructions wrong."

I stared at him for a long moment and he stared right back. Maybe I didn't know him that well, but something about his eyes just then made my stomach squirm.

"No way," I said, pushing myself up off the bed. "You knew about this all along, didn't you?"

"What?" Ian blurted, his jaw dropping.

"You did! This was all just your little plan to get me into bed!" I said, my face growing red. "Oh, my God. How stupid am I?"

"Layla, you're losing it," Ian said, getting up on his knees and edging toward me. "There was no plan, I swear. You're not the stupid one, I am. I'm a stupid git. But I'm not some insane lothario using rock stars' apartments to woo women."

I crossed my arms over my chest. "Sure looks that way to me."

"Come on," Ian said, standing up in front of me. His T-shirt had long since been shed and his six-pack abs would have looked mighty fine right then if I wasn't so mad. "Think about this logically. When you said you didn't want to have sex, I was totally fine with it. Did I once try to push you into doing something you didn't want to do?" he asked, looking me straight in the eye.

"No," I said reluctantly.

"So would a guy bent on bedding you be the total gentleman I was tonight?" he asked.

I stared at him. He did have a point. "No. I guess not."

"All right," he said, putting his hands on my shoulders. "So why don't you just go back to sleep, and just to show you how sorry I am, I will go sleep out in the game room?"

I sighed and let my shoulder muscles uncoil. "That's okay. We can both stay in here," I said. "I mean, the bed *is* the size of Wisconsin."

Ian laughed, and pulled me in and gave me a kiss on the forehead. "You're one of a kind, Layla Carter," he said.

"Yeah. I am," I replied. Then I turned toward the bed, more than ready to sink back into its luxuriousness. "Wait a minute. What about Necro?" I said.

"Eh, don't worry about him. He never comes home before dawn on the night of a concert," Ian said, crawling toward the pillows.

Once again, a little sliver of doubt entered my mind. If he knew that, and if he *did* know the party was at Rodrigo's, he would have known he would have me here alone all night long. Was he really just a "stupid git," or was he a fabulous schemer?

I slid under the covers and turned my back to him, holding the silk sheet up to my chin.

"Good night, Ian," I said.

"Night, Lay-la-la," he sang.

Then, within minutes, he dozed off again while I lay awake for hours, staring at one of the Bloodworms's gold records, wondering what I had gotten myself into.

The next morning I woke up alone in Necro Phillips's bed. I dressed quickly and walked out into the living room/dining room/bar area and found Ian sitting at the glass-topped dining table in front of a spread that would have made Henry the Eighth drool. There was a huge fruit platter, a plate of French toast, eggs and bacon, a dozen bagels, and pretty much every jam known to man.

"Don't tell me you cook," I joked.

"Uh, no," Ian replied. "Necro has a personal chef. She's in the kitchen right now."

"You had his chef cook for us?" I asked, feeling a little unworthy.

"Believe me, Greta was glad to do it," Ian said, munching on a piece of bacon. "Necro eats nothing but beef jerky and M&Ms. The woman was dying to put her talents to work."

He watched me as I hesitated behind one of the chairs. Everything looked amazing, but it just felt a little too weird. I'd never had a personal chef cook for me before. I was in someone else's house with some guy who didn't live there, putting the help to work. It was a tad surreal.

"She'll be insulted if you don't eat," he said. "Come on. Tuck in."

"Well, if you insist," I said, pulling out a chair. I helped myself to some of the French toast and fruit and took a bite. It tasted even better than it looked. Between the food and the view of the city, I felt like I'd just won the lottery.

Now if I could just figure out the hot guy and whether he was or was not a player, everything might all fall into place.

"It's beautiful, isn't it?" Ian asked, glancing out at the sun-streaked high-rises.

"Yeah. I could get used to this," I teased.

"Well, if I have anything to say about it, we'll be doing these things more often," Ian replied, popping a strawberry into his mouth.

I grinned, enjoying the moment. "Sounds good to me."

Ian's cell phone rang and he glanced at the caller ID. "It's my dad," he said, picking it up.

I tried not to eavesdrop. I really did. But Ian was right there, and he was talking about the Bloodworms. My face completely overheated when I heard him say, "Yeah. We'll meet you there. Tell Necro thanks for letting us crash." Then there was a pause. "All right, all right. I'll tell him myself."

172

Ian hung up the phone and smiled at me. "Looks like you'll be officially meeting the band after all. That is, if you don't mind spending the day in the city."

"Mind? Are you kidding?" I said.

"Good. Then I can make last night's travesty up to you," Ian said.

"You don't have to make anything up to me," I told him.

"Oh, no? I guess I'll just call them and cancel, then," he said, flipping open his cell phone.

I grabbed it away and held it out of his reach. "No! Don't you dare!"

Ian laughed. "Well, come on then. We'll have to go shopping."

"Shopping? Why?" I asked, scrambling up.

"We'll be meeting them for lunch at one of these swank downtown eateries," Ian told me. "You don't want to be meeting the Bloodworms in your grimy clothes from last night, do you?"

I lifted my T-shirt to my nose and grimaced. He had a point. I smelled like sweat from dancing and cigarette smoke from the girls that had been behind us at the show.

"But I don't have any money," I said, following Ian to the door.

"Not a problem," he said, whipping out a credit card. "It's on Dad."

I stopped in my tracks. I can't say I wasn't tempted. But this seemed a little, I don't know, *wrong*?

"No way," I objected. "I don't know when I could pay him back."

Ian was already grabbing his leather jacket and heading for the door. "Don't even think about it. Dad is always free with the currency when we're out on tour. He won't even notice."

I hesitated as I slid my arms into my own jacket. "Ian—"

"Come on, Layla. I want to do this. It'll be a blast," he said. "Besides, I fancy a change of clothing myself."

I had a feeling I wasn't going to talk him out of this. And besides, who really wanted to? We were talking a free shopping spree in NYC and I *am* an American female.

"All right," I said finally. "Let's spend."

Before I knew it, Ian and I were strolling down a cobblestone street in Lower Manhattan, window shopping our way from trendy store to trendy store. Each shop had more gorgeous things than the next, but I had a feeling that if I had been on my own, I wouldn't have been able to afford so much as a pair of socks in most of them. Finally, Ian chose a smallish boutique with a plain, purple square for a sign. I checked out a pair of ripped and patched jeans right at the front of the store when we entered.

Three-hundred and twenty-five dollars. I felt like clutching my purse and running for the nearest Gap.

Ian approached the counter and the tiny, Asian woman working the register completely lit up at the sight of him.

"Ian! Good to see you! How's your dad?" she asked.

"Hello, Kiyoko," Ian said, giving her a kiss on both cheeks. "Dad is still rockin' with the Worms, as always. Actually, we're lunching with the band. This is my friend,

Layla," he said, gesturing to me. "We need to hook her up with a Necro-worthy outfit."

Kiyoko looked at me and smiled. "Oh, with a gorgeous girl like this, dressing her should be no problem."

I blushed. Hard. "Thank you."

"Here. Let's get you to a dressing room and I will pick out some things for you," Kiyoko said, bustling me behind an orange curtain. "Get undressed. I'll be right back."

"Uh . . . okay," I said, as she snatched the curtain closed in front of my face.

I kind of wanted to browse around myself, but I didn't want to tell her how to run her store. I sat down on the tiny bench and waited. This might be better anyway. There's no way I'd be comfortable picking out three-hundred-dollar jeans for myself.

"Here you go, love," Ian said, handing a few things around the curtain for me. "Kiyoko picked it herself."

I took the jeans, dark blue with leather patches on the pockets, and pulled them on. They fit perfectly and made my ass look amazing. Then I slipped a buttery, black, cashmere shell over my head. It had a funky beaded appliqué on the right shoulder and screamed upscale rock star. I looked incredible, but when I checked the price tag, I almost hurled.

"So? Let's see?" Ian said.

I opened the curtain and Ian smiled slowly. "You look stunning."

"Thanks," I said. "But Ian. It's too much. I could sell half my wardrobe and still not be able to afford this."

"Layla, please. Don't worry about it," Ian said, taking my hands. "You get what you pay for. And trust me. That outfit is worth it."

"Well, if you're sure," I said, biting my lip.

"Oh. I'm sure."

He looked me up and down like he just couldn't take his eyes off me and I shivered, feeling beautiful and pampered and special. Finally, I grinned.

"Sold?" Ian said.

I nodded. "Sold."

A couple hours and half a dozen shops later, Ian and I walked into the swank restaurant looking like rock stars ourselves. Ian had picked out a black turtleneck and striped pants for himself and we had both splurged on reflective sunglasses. I actually saw a couple heads turn as we walked by.

"There's Dad," Ian said, lifting his chin.

My stomach did an excited pirouette when we spotted the table. Ian's father was surrounded by Bloodworms. All five of them were there, kicked back, sipping their drinks and chatting loudly. The band members were rumpled and clearly spent, their hair scraggly, and their clothes thrown on. They looked as if they'd just woken up enough to crawl into the restaurant. And still, they looked amazing. They were rock stars. They could get away with it. Everyone else in the restaurant was trying not to gawk at them.

"Guess we didn't need to go to all this effort," I said, looking down at my pristine outfit.

"I didn't do it for them. I did it for you," Ian said squeezing my hand as we crossed the restaurant.

Well. This day just got better and better.

"Good morning, all," Ian said as we arrived at the table.

My heart pounded almost painfully in my chest. These were the Bloodworms. I was about to have lunch with the Bloodworms. Would Necro remember me from the power circle the night before? Should I say something or would that sound too stalker-esque? Oh, God. I didn't think this through.

"Don't you two look spry," remarked Necro, gazing up blearily from his panini. "Apparently you were having such a good time, you didn't bother to come to the party."

"We meant to, but we called it an early night instead," Ian said, pulling out a chair for me to sit.

"I see," Necro said suggestively.

I blushed painfully. What was Necro Phillips implying?

Ian shot Necro a look of death. "Back off, Necro."

Whoa. Unbelievable. Ian was comfortable enough with these guys to tell Necro off? To defend my honor to him? Could he be any cooler?

I smiled as I sat. "Hi, Mr. Cramer," I said, considering he A) was the only person there I had officially met and B) had, unbeknownst to him, just bought me a hugely expensive outfit.

"Hello, Layla," he said pleasantly. "I'd like you to meet the band. This is Necro, Rodrigo—"

"Tommy, Norton, and Cash," I finished. "I know." I smiled sheepishly. "I'm a big fan." A couple of them chuckled while Cash raised his bushy eyebrows at me. "Oh, God. I sound like a loser. Can we strike that from the record?"

"We would, but we like to meet fans," Rodrigo said, shaking my hand over the table.

"Thanks," I replied, feeling a tad more comfortable.

"So? If you're such a big fan, what are your favorite songs?" Necro asked.

Actually, it sounded more like a challenge. I glanced at Ian, who shrugged.

"Uh, well. I love 'Failed.' But I've always wondered if it's about the environment or the peace movement," I said.

I couldn't believe I was getting to ask the actual band about this. I wished Cara was there. She would have died to be sitting next to me just then.

"Well, that's a good question, isn't it?" Rodrigo said. "I think it's about what you want it to be about. That's the point of music, isn't it? It touches each listener in a different way."

"Actually, it was about the third time I tried to quit smoking," Necro said, staring me in the eye.

My heart sank. "Really?"

"Now why'd you have to go and tell the girl that?" Rodrigo asked him, taking a slug of his drink. "You'll spoil our image."

"Like I've ever cared about image," Necro said with a sniff.

I squirmed a bit and looked at Ian. He shook his head like he was irritated at a little brother or something.

"What about 'Pet Peeve'?" I asked, trying again. "Is that

about animal testing?"

"Yes, it is," Rodrigo said, leaning forward. "You know, most people don't get that. That's very astute of you to—"

"Actually, I wrote that song because I was pissed at Carter for putting his hamster on my head while I was asleep," Necro said, leaning back in his chair and staring me down. "Don't try to find meaning in every song, girlie. Not everything is so deep."

I felt like I had been slapped. Was Necro always this mean, or did I just bring it out in him?

"All right, that's it," Ian said, standing. "We're going."

"Going, huh? Seems to be a theme with you, mate," Necro said.

I looked from Ian to Necro and back again. "Okay, what is going on here?" I said.

"I'll tell you what's going on," Necro replied, sitting forward and looking me sharply in the eye. "Thanks to you my little sister is sitting back in London right now with a broken heart."

"What?" I asked, baffled.

"I don't believe this!" Ian said. "She's the one who broke up with me! Did she tell you she took up with Hugh the moment I left the country, or did she neglect to mention that?"

"You saying my baby sister is a liar?" Necro demanded, rising from his chair.

Whoa. This could not mean what I thought it meant.

"This is not going to be pretty," Rodrigo said under his breath.

"Wait a minute, wait a minute," I said, my pulse racing. "Alexandra? Alexandra is Necro's *sister*?"

"Yeah," Ian said. "And she's the one who busted up with me. So I would appreciate it if you would back off my friend."

"Your friend, huh? You always spend entire nights with your friends in other people's flats?" Necro demanded.

"If you were so put off about it, why did you let me use it?" Ian asked.

"I had no idea you *were* using it! Or believe me, I would have thrown you out myself, you tosser!" Necro spat.

"All right. That's enough," Ian's father said, standing. He glanced over his shoulder where I noticed the restaurant manager eyeing us with disdain. "Ian, maybe you should just go."

Ian clucked his tongue. "But, Da—"

"Layla, I apologize," his father said, taking out his cell phone. "I'll call you two a car to take you back to Kensington."

"Oh. Okay," I said, rising shakily out of my chair. I picked up my purse and the shopping bag that held my old clothes. "It was . . . nice to meet you," I said to no one in particular.

Rodrigo shot me a sympathetic, apologetic look as I turned away. At least one member of my favorite band was an actual human.

"There will be a limo outside in ten minutes," Ian's father said as we passed by him. He grabbed Ian's arm and leaned toward his ear. "I told you not to get involved with that girl. Didn't I tell you it was only going to cause problems?"

It took me a moment to realize he was talking about Alexandra, not me. I looked at Ian, who stared his father in the eye.

"Well, it's over now, isn't it?" he said. "It's not my fault some people never grow up," he said, shooting a look at Necro. Then he turned and took my hand. "Come on, Layla."

And just like that, my big meeting with the Bloodworms was over.

In the plush limo on the way home, I stared out at the passing trees, cuddled up into the crook of Ian's arm. I couldn't believe everything that had happened. Necro Phillips had gotten into a fight about me. Ian had taken on Necro on my behalf. After a night of doubting whether or not Ian was serious about me, I was fairly certain now that he was. What guy would bring a girl to lunch with his ex's brother if he wasn't serious about the girl? Why go to all that trouble unless it was for real?

"Thanks for defending me back there," I said.

"I'm just sorry I put you through that," Ian told me. "I thought Necro was over it."

"It's okay," I said, lifting my chin to look at him. "You didn't know. I had a great time with *you*, though. Last night, this morning. All and all, it was a blast."

Ian smirked. "Yeah. Getting berated by rock stars in public must have been a dream come true."

"Hey. At least it was interesting," I said with a shrug.

"But you? You are definitely a dream come true."

"Oh, Lay-la-la," he said teasingly, wrapping a curl of my hair around his finger. Then he leaned in and kissed me and the rest of the ride back home passed in a flash.

fifteen

"Omigod, Cara, it was amazing," I said as we sat down in a booth at Johnny's on Sunday night. "I *wish* you had been there."

"So do I," Cara said, wide-eyed. "That was *definitely* worth missing the dance for. In fact, just that outfit was worth missing the dance for," she added, reaching out to finger the cashmere sweater. I hadn't taken it off all day.

"I know," I replied. "Ian was like a dream. I feel bad that I ever doubted him."

Cara sighed dreamily. "A true international romance. Who would have thunk it?"

Then her face fell as she looked at the door.

"What?" I asked, already turning around.

Nate Henry had just walked in and he had his hand on

the small of Jenny Morrison's back. She giggled at something he said and he led her right over to the booth just behind ours. He went a little ashen when he saw us sitting there, but Jenny smiled at us triumphantly and bounced into her seat. Suddenly I found it hard to swallow.

"Are they, like, together now?" I whispered to Cara.

"He took her to the dance last minute," Cara confirmed. "But what do you care? You have Ian."

At that moment my cell phone rang. I checked the caller ID and my irritation was replaced by exhilaration. "Speaking of . . ."

"Hi, Ian," I said into the phone. Maybe a bit loudly. Not that I *wanted* Nate and Jenny to hear, but—

Okay. Maybe I did.

"Hey, Lay-la-la," he said smoothly. "I wanted to let you know I won't be in school tomorrow. Just in case you were going to worry about me."

"Oh," I said, disappointed. "What are you up to?"

"I'm gonna help my dad with some stuff, but don't fret. I *will* be seeing you," he told me.

"How's that, exactly?" I asked with a grin.

"Because you are going to accompany me to a press party for the Skulls tomorrow night," he said.

"The who?" I asked.

"No, not the Who. The Skulls," Ian joked.

I laughed. "I've never heard of them."

"It's a band headed up by Rodrigo's little brother. They're absolutely fab," he said. "And the party is at the Treetop Club."

"You're kidding," I said, my jaw dropping.

Cara looked at me, intrigued. "What?" she whispered.

I placed my hand over the receiver. "He wants to take me to the Treetop Club!" I whispered back, my feet tapping under the table.

"Oh, my God!" she hissed.

"I know!"

The Treetop was the trendiest club in Westchester County. No one I knew had ever actually gotten in there, though many had tried.

"How are we supposed to get in?" I asked Ian.

We were, after all, a bit shy of twenty-one.

"Leave that to me," he replied. "Pick you up at seven?"

"I'll be ready," I told him.

Then I hung up the phone and Cara and I both squealed. Who cared about Nate Henry and Jenny "dumb-blonde" Morrison? I was going to the Treetop Club with Ian Cramer. My life could not possibly get any better.

Monday night I found myself, once again, being shuttled through the back door by a mega-bouncer, this one named Truck. (I'm doubting his mother gave him that name.) Truck had a purple Mohawk and a skull tattoo on his forearm. Oddly, he was also one of the most polite people I had met in my life. Appearances can definitely be deceiving.

"I'll find one of the waitresses and send her over," Truck told us, after escorting Ian and me to a table in the corner marked RESERVED. The club was even cooler than I had imagined. The ceiling was completely covered with faux branches and leaves, with strobe lights peeking through here and there to flash on the dance floor. The bases of the tables looked like tree trunks and the benches and chairs were covered in thick, moss-colored velvet. They had definitely taken their theme to the extreme.

"Thanks, Truck," I said, taking in the crowd. Everyone was talking at the top of their voices and glancing every so often at the stage, anticipating the arrival of the Skulls.

"No need to thank me," he said, flashing a gold-toothed smile. "You two enjoy yourselves."

"What did I tell you?" Ian asked as Truck moved off, people jumping out of his way as he passed.

"You're good," I told him. "No one even mentioned an ID."

"Stick with me, Lay-la-la," he said, leaning in for a smooch. "You'll go places."

I laughed and turned my attention to the front of the club as the Skulls were announced. The crowd went berserk as the guys took the stage. They were a little more clean-cut and fresh-faced than the Bloodworms and I liked their music. Their name may have sounded foreboding, but their tunes were upbeat and danceable, and soon Ian was pulling me onto the dance floor.

He was, of course, an incredible dancer. I guess that's what growing up around professional musicians will do for you. We danced nonstop for eight songs until my hair was plastered to my face and neck with sweat.

"I think we should take a break," I told Ian as one particularly fast song came to an end.

"Sure," Ian said, breathless. "Let's get a drink."

"Oy! Is that Ian Cramer I see in the crowd?" a voice said through the sound system.

Ian and I paused. He turned slowly toward the stage and raised a hand. "You caught me, Dom. How are you?"

"All right," Dom, the lead singer, said as everyone turned to stare at us. "Why don't you come on up here and strap on a guitar?"

I turned to Ian, stunned. "You play?"

"A little," he said.

"Don't be a skittish git!" Dom shouted. "Get up here!"

A few people in the crowd started to clap a steady beat, urging Ian on.

"Do you mind if I go?" he asked.

"Are you kidding?" I said excitedly. "This I gotta see!"

Ian kissed my cheek, then bounded for the stage. This was surreal. He was gorgeous, he treated me like a queen, *and* he was a musician? I couldn't have dreamed up a more perfect guy!

Ian climbed onto the stage, grabbed a guitar, and he and Dom whispered a few words to each other. Then they launched into the next song together. Ian looked like a professional up there. Totally natural. Like jamming with the band was something he did all the time.

And damn was it sexy.

"Your boyfriend is *so* hot," a random redheaded girl shouted as she danced nearby.

"Thanks!" I shouted back.

Boyfriend, huh? Interesting. As I watched Ian play, my

187

heart started to pound harder and harder. He was born to be in the spotlight. He clearly loved it and everyone in the crowd clearly loved him. Ian Cramer. My boyfriend.

My boyfriend is with the band.

I could get used to that.

The next two weeks spun by like a crazy kaleidoscope of constant motion. Club-hopping, hanging with bands, dancing with Ian, stealing kisses backstage or in the backseats of limousines. I felt like a rock star, myself.

And I was getting about as much sleep as a rock star, too. Luckily, my mother was pretty cool about it. She had always treated me like an adult and now she was no different. As long as my grades didn't start to suffer, she would be fine.

So when I got a D back on my latest Trig quiz, I felt a lump of foreboding form in my stomach.

"How'd you do?" Cara asked, snatching the quiz out of my hand as we walked out of class. Her mouth dropped open. "A D? Layla!"

"It's just one D," I grumbled as we reached my locker. I grabbed the paper back and crumpled it, wishing I could crumple away my disappointment as well. "Besides, we're seniors. It's not like it matters."

"Layla, what's going on with you?" Cara asked, leaning against the row of lockers. "I feel like we haven't really talked in days. And, no offense, but you look exhausted."

I took a deep breath and let it out noisily.

"I am kind of tired," I said. I popped my locker open

and looked in the magnetic mirror. What I saw there was not pretty. Pale skin, a big zit on my cheek from falling asleep with my makeup on one too many times, and dark circles under my eyes.

"Ew. I see what you mean," I admitted.

"Are you okay?" she asked.

"I'm fine," I told her, smiling. "Just in desperate need of a facial."

"Layla—"

"Cara," I said, mimicking her concerned tone. "Ian and I are having so much fun. And yeah, maybe that means I haven't been getting much sleep, but it's totally worth it. Ian is the best thing that's ever happened to me."

"If you say so," Cara said noncommittally.

"Wow. Way to be supportive," I said.

"I'm sorry, it's just . . . I'm worried about you, okay? I've never seen a guy change you like this before. I mean, you've missed two meetings for the newspaper. Did you even know that Mr. Harris made us take the Kensington Daze down?"

"Good riddance," I muttered.

"You haven't handed in an article in weeks, and—"

"Is that what this is really about?" I snapped. "The paper? It's just a school paper, Cara. I can miss a couple of issues."

"See!?" she said, standing up straight. "The Layla I know would never have said that."

I blinked and instantly guilt started to seep through my veins. She was right. The Layla *I* knew never would have said that either.

189

"I'm sorry," I said, rubbing my forehead. "I'll get back on track. Just . . . give me a little time."

"Hey, Lay-la-la!"

We both turned at the sound of Ian's deep voice. He stepped past Cara and wrapped me up in his strong arms. Instantly, everything inside of me relaxed and I melted into his kiss. Ah. Exactly what I needed. A good Ian fix.

"Hey, Layla's friend," he greeted Cara with a smile.

She rolled her eyes and turned around. "On that note," she said, walking away.

My face warmed, embarrassed.

"It's really about time you learn her name," I told Ian.

"Why? You're the only one I care about," he said, trailing a finger down my cheek.

I grinned, blushing now for a whole other reason. Then Ian's cell phone beeped and he yanked it out of his pocket. He glanced at the screen and his face completely changed.

"What's wrong?" I asked.

Ian quickly pocketed the phone. "Nothing. Why should anything be wrong?"

"You just looked a little freaked," I pointed out.

"Hey, do you know what I really dig about you, Lay-la-la?" he said.

"What?" I asked.

"You're such fun," he replied. "Just free and easy fun. You're not like other birds who make everything a big to-do. You really know how to kick back and not worry about what stuff 'means' all the time. You know what I mean?"

My heart thumped extra hard. Something about his attitude shift was disconcerting, but I couldn't put my finger on it.

"Sure," I said tentatively.

"I'd better get to class," he said. "Catch you later."

Then he turned and walked off without so much as a cheek kiss. Something was obviously up with him. Or maybe I was just too exhausted to process anything. Either way it wasn't like me not to get an answer out of him before letting him walk away.

Maybe Cara was right. Maybe I *had* changed. Or maybe it was just time for me to get some sleep.

sixteen

"Listen, I know we were supposed to go to the Treetop tonight, but something has come up, and I can't make it," Ian said on the phone that weekend. "I'm sorry, love."

Funny, but he didn't sound sorry to me. In fact, he was sounding sort of upbeat.

"Oh. I was really looking forward to it," I told him.

Ian blew out a sigh. "I said I was sorry, Layla. I do have responsibilities."

"Well, excuse me," I said sarcastically. "Didn't realize I was dealing with your uptight side."

"You know, I really don't need a guilt trip right now," Ian said snappishly. "Ring me when you quit PMS-ing."

With that, the line went dead.

All righty then. Talk about overreacting.

So much for our free and breezy relationship. Apparently I wasn't even allowed to be disappointed. In my experience, when guys turned a person's feelings around on them like that it could only mean one thing: He was up to something.

I knew it. I knew I hadn't been imagining things in the hall the other day. And now that I'd had a few nights of solid sleep I was more sure of that than ever.

I hit the speed-dial button for Cara and held my breath while it rang.

"Hey, Layla," she said.

"Hey. You up for a little reconnaissance?" I said.

"Always," she replied instantly. "Who are we stalking?"

I laughed. "Not stalking. Just . . . fact finding," I said. "Pick me up in an hour. And wear something funky."

"Why? Where are we going?" she asked.

"The Treetop," I said. "I have a sneaking suspicion there's going to be a surprise appearance tonight."

"We're never going to get in," Cara said as we strode across the packed parking lot. She was a good few feet behind me, not as comfortable in high heels as I was.

"Don't worry about it. I know people," I told her, flicking my hair over my shoulder.

"Oh, well then, your highness. Lead on," she mocked, rolling her eyes.

I smiled and executed Ian's secret knock on the back door of the Treetop. I was trying my best to act confident, but inside I was a mess of psychotically moshing butterflies. If I was right, if Ian *was* here and he had just blown me off, I wasn't sure what I was going to do. All I knew was I had to find out. I was not one for getting played.

The door opened and Truck smiled out at us. He was wearing a pair of denim overalls with nothing on under them. I felt Cara tense as he flashed his gold tooth.

"Hi, Truck," I said, lifting my chin.

"Layla! Welcome back!" he said, opening the door wide.

"This is my friend Cara," I said.

"Pleasure to meet you," he said, offering his hand.

Cara shook it tentatively. "You, too," she said, shooting me a look.

"Is Ian here already?" I asked Truck casually.

Truck nodded and my heart took a nosedive. "Sure is. Want me to show you to his table?"

"No thanks," I told him, feeling ill. "I know where it is." Cara and I started down the hall toward the club and my chest pounded right along with the dance music pumping inside. "I knew it," I said through my teeth. "I knew he was lying."

"Just stay calm," she told me, touching my arm comfortingly. "Maybe he had a good reason."

"Since when are you on his side?" I asked.

"I'm not. You know I'm not," Cara told me calmly. "I just don't want you to freak out."

We paused at the edge of the dance floor and I looked toward Ian's usual table. The crowd parted and I saw him.

He was right there, twenty yards away, practically touching noses with some leggy blonde in a black halter dress.

Kick me in the head, why don't you?

"Oh, my God," I said under my breath. "I'm going to *kill* him." I stalked across the dance floor, practically shoving the clubbers aside as I went.

"See, this is what I was trying to avoid!" Cara shouted, scurrying after me.

The moment I arrived at Ian's table I pulled out an extra chair and sat down. Ian blanched when he saw me. Blond Girl just looked confused. Cara nervously pulled out a fourth chair and sat down a safe distance away.

"Hi!" I said, reaching out my hand to the blonde. "Who are you?"

"Uh . . . I'm Alexandra," she said with a thick British accent. "And you are?"

"Oh! Alexandra, huh?" I said, my blood boiling. I looked at Ian and he stared down at the candle on the table. "I'm Layla. I'm the girl that was supposed to come here with Ian tonight."

"Alex, we should go—" Ian said, starting to get up.

"Layla," Alexandra said flatly, not moving a muscle. Ian fell back down into his seat. Clearly she recognized my name. "This is Layla?" she said, turning to Ian. "You said she was fat. You said she was fat and lonely and you felt sorry for her."

"What?" I blurted.

"He took you to my brother's concert, right?" she said. "He said you were a charity case."

I liked this girl. Clearly she wasn't afraid to speak the

195

truth. Kind of like someone else I knew.

"Really?" I said, staring Ian down. "Do you always take charity cases back to rock stars' apartments to seduce them?"

"Layla," Ian said, cornered. He looked at Alexandra. "She's lying, baby," he said, begging. "She's been following me around this entire time. Practically stalking me."

"*What?*" I blurted. "You were the one who pursued me!"

"How long has this been going on, Ian?" Alexandra asked, standing up and crossing her arms over her chest. "How long have you been lying to me?"

"Wait a minute," he said, sliding to the end of the bench. "You're the one who took up with my best friend, remember?"

"Yes. And I've apologized for that," Alexandra said. "I told you I was wrong and you forgave me two weeks ago. I put together this whole trip to come see you and now I find out you've been fooling around with a supermodel behind my back."

A supermodel? Wow. I *really* liked this girl.

"Alex, you know you're the only girl I've ever wanted. The only girl I've ever loved," Ian said, stepping toward her.

Ouch. Can't say that one didn't sting a little. Alex rolled her eyes and looked away.

"God, Layla! Why are you doing this to me?" Ian blurted, frustrated. "You knew we weren't serious!"

"Excuse me? I did not know that!" I said. "I mean, I know we didn't start out that way, but, you know, we've been spending all this time together. I thought—"

Ian scoffed. "Please. Everyone knows you're just a good time girl. That's your thing. You can't tell me you actually *wanted* a relationship."

"Oh, so this was just about sex?" Alexandra interjected. "That makes me feel *so* much better!"

"No! It was not about sex!" I told her, standing now as well. "We never even *had* sex."

Wait a minute, why was I yelling at her? I turned back to Ian, about ready to explode.

"What the hell do you mean, 'a good time girl'?"

"I read the Kensington Daze. I know what you're about," Ian replied derisively.

"Oh, my God!" I shouted. "Are you kidding me? You *believed* that crap?"

"Well, I did. For a bit. Until you kept refusing to give it up," he said with a laugh.

"*What?*" Alexandra shouted.

Ian started as if he'd forgotten she was there.

"Not that I was trying to get her to give it up—" he hedged.

Unbelievable. This guy was unbelievable. He thought he was this sly player but, in fact, he was a total idiot. I turned around and grabbed his drink from the table behind me. Then, on impulse, I grabbed Alexandra's, too, and handed it to her.

"I don't know about you, Alex, but there's something I've always wanted to do," I said.

Alex looked at me, looked at the drink in her hand, then smiled.

"What?" Ian said warily.

"This," I said.

Then Alex and I tossed both of the drinks in his face at once. Cara burst out laughing and the people all around us applauded. Ian's face dripped with scotch and apple martini. To his credit, he just stood there and took it like a man. He didn't even try to wipe himself down.

"Nice meeting you," I said to Alexandra. "I wish you a nice life."

"You, too," she said with a smile.

She grabbed her purse and then we both took off in opposite directions, Alex for the front door, Cara and I for the back.

"That was awesome!" Cara said as we blew past Truck.

"You leaving already?" Truck asked, spreading his arms wide.

"We'll be back someday," I told him, blowing him an air kiss.

We shoved our way out into the cold night and I took a deep breath. Sometimes a good breakup—one I was totally positively sure about—felt even better than a good kiss.

Ian Cramer was such a colossal waste of time. I felt sorry for the poor girl who ended up with him. At that moment, I couldn't have been happier that it wasn't going to be me.

"How do you feel?" Cara asked, stepping up next to me.

"I feel good," I told her honestly. "I feel . . . free."

Then my stomach rumbled loudly and we both laughed. There was that breakup symptom again: the intense junk food craving.

"So, ice cream?" she suggested, slipping her arm through mine.

"Ice cream," I said with a nod.

No matter what, there were three people in this world I could *always* rely on: Cara, Ben, and Jerry.

The End

The Choice Redux

Well . . . *that* could have turned out better, don't you think? Now, do me a favor and go back to page 103 and try again.

You Chose Drew

twelve

"Okay. Why am I even thinking about this?" I said finally, taking a deep breath. "There's really only one answer to this dilemma."

"I knew it," Cara said, brightening. "Nate, right? You're going with Nate?"

"Uh, no!" I said, picking up my phone. "Cara, I finally, *finally* have a shot with Drew Sullivan. No offense, but that's worth a thousand Nate Henrys."

Cara's shoulders slumped, but she nodded. "You *have* been obsessing about him for years."

"See? Sorry I won't be going to the dance with you, but a stalker has to do what a stalker has to do," I told her, patting her on the shoulder.

"Okay," she said reluctantly, picking up her purse. "I

guess I'll go pick up Mike, then." She started for the door, then paused and turned back to me. "But when you see Drew, I'd avoid using the word *stalker*."

I smiled. "Thanks for the tip."

Before she was out the door, I was already dialing Nate. I held my breath as the phone rang. Poor guy was probably already all dressed up in his suit and ready to go. I just hoped he wasn't *too* heartbroken.

But then, there was also the possibility that he might be sitting there getting ready to break up with me. So maybe he wouldn't be heartbroken at all.

Just get it over with, I told myself. *Then you can go out and have a little fun. With Drew Sullivan!*

"Hey, Layla!" Nate said when he picked up the phone. "How are you feeling?"

Uh-oh. He sounded happy. Like a guy more than psyched to go to a dance. I took a deep breath and braced myself. This was not going to be pretty.

By the time I heard Drew's motorcycle roar up the street an hour later, I was a giddy, nervous wreck. Neither Nate nor Ian had taken my last-minute ditch very well, which hadn't helped my nerves. Now all I wanted was for this date to start so I could relax already.

As if I'd ever be able to relax around Drew.

It seemed like it took forever for him to walk up the driveway and ring the bell. When I whipped the door open he was obviously startled.

Huh. Maybe I should have counted to ten Mississippis.

"Hey," he said, looking me quickly up and down.

"Hi."

I waited for the compliment I knew was coming. After all, I had outdone myself with the dramatic makeup and the stylish upsweep of the hair. Plus my halter top exposed just the tiniest sliver of my stomach—and the belly-button ring that so turned Drew on. I was in rare form.

"So. Ready to go?" he said, turning toward the driveway impatiently.

"Oh. Yeah," I said.

So much for that compliment. I grabbed my black leather jacket and slammed the door behind us. Maybe he was just nervous about the show. Yeah. That had to be it.

He straddled his bike and I took the extra helmet and climbed on behind him. For a long moment I stared at the helmet and hesitated. Crap. Why hadn't I thought of this when I was doing my hair?

"Better put that on," Drew prompted me.

I grimaced. Guess there was a drawback to dating a guy with a bike. But then, this was Drew Sullivan. I could suffer a bad-hair night for him. I bit my lip and yanked the helmet down over my head, feeling my 'do crush against my skull.

"Ready?" he asked, revving the engine.

"Ready!" I replied.

As I wrapped my arms around him and settled in for the ride, I decided to just forget about the creaky beginning. I was out with Drew Sullivan on Valentine's night. He had asked me to view his work, which was very personal for him. I just had to relax and go with the flow. This was going to be an incredible date.

Two hours later I was hiding a yawning fit behind my champagne glass and trying as hard as I could not to check my watch for the twenty-fifth time. I couldn't help it. Never in my life had I been surrounded by so many uptight, pretentious people. And it wasn't like I hadn't *tried* to make conversation with some of the art-lovers Drew had introduced me to, it was just that every time I opened my mouth they looked at me like I was the crud on the crunchy crudités that were being passed around.

What *was* that mush anyway?

I sighed as Drew wrapped up a conversation with another stuffy white-haired man in a suit. At least he was chatting with *someone*. I, however, had been ignored most of the night. For the past hour I had been trying to figure out why Drew had even brought me to this place. Okay, so seeing his artwork displayed on those stark white walls among the work of other talented painters had been incredible—for about ten minutes. Since then the only thing that had kept me awake had been pondering whether or not Drew remembered I was there.

Finally, he approached me.

"Hey," he said quietly, rejoining me in the corner I had staked out for myself. "See that guy over there?"

"Yeah?" I said, trying not to sound too bored.

"He just bought one of my pieces," Drew said, grinning.

"No way!" I whispered. "Drew, that's amazing."

"I know," he said, taking a deep breath. "Look, you want to get out of here?"

"Really?" I asked hopefully. "You sure you don't want to mingle some more?"

"I'm not much of a mingler," he replied. "I just wanted to see how the stuff was received, you know?"

Wow. For the first time all night Drew was actually uttering more than two words to me. I could have kissed that old man for buying his painting.

"Yeah, I know," I told him. "Okay. Let's get our jackets."

Out on the street I held my jacket close to my skin and followed Drew over to his bike, feeling giddy once more. Now our date could really get started.

"So, where are we headed?" I asked.

Drew looked at me as he pulled his helmet on. "I thought I'd take you home."

Wha-huh? My spirits completely drooped.

"Home? Why?"

Drew shrugged. "Didn't really have anything else planned," he said.

"Oh."

What the hell kind of date was this? Was it just me or had he just taken me to a business meeting? I didn't get the chance to ask because he was already on his bike, cranking the engine up.

"Hop on," he shouted.

I took my helmet and reluctantly crawled on behind him. As we headed back toward my house my mind whirled. This was unacceptable. I hadn't even had a chance to flirt with him, to talk to him, to find out anything more about him or tell him anything more about me. What if this was my last chance with Drew? What if he walked away from this date thinking I was utterly boring just because I hadn't been able to make small talk with those art jerks and had hid out all night? Had I just entirely blown it?

Drew pulled into my driveway and kept the engine running. He wasn't even leaving open the possibility of coming inside. I had to figure out a way to hold his interest. I had to at least get a second date out of this—another chance.

"So," I said nervously, swinging my leg over the rear of the bike and placing the helmet back in its holder.

"So," he replied. "Thanks for coming."

"Yeah. No problem," I said. "It was fun."

He didn't take his helmet off. He wasn't even going to kiss me. What was with this guy? One day he was mauling me on a piercing table and the next he was giving me the cold-as-ice vibe.

"Well. See ya," he said, starting to roll backward.

"Wait!"

Drew stopped and looked quizzically at me. An idea had been forming at the back of my mind all the way home, but I had ignored it, thinking it was too crazy. Now, however, faced with the idea of him driving off and my never seeing him again, it seemed like my only shot.

"What's up?" he asked.

"I was wondering if you'd design a tattoo for me," I blurted.

Drew placed his feet on the ground and killed the

engine. He pulled his helmet off and shook his hair out. Ah,
bliss.

"Really?" he said.

Seemed I did know how to get his attention.

thirteen

The next day I sat at a window table at Starbucks, watching Drew weave his way toward me with our drinks. He sat down and placed my latte in front of me, then pulled the lid off his steaming hot coffee and took a sip.

"Thanks," I said, flipping my hair over my shoulder with a smile. Okay, so I was posing. I had to remind this guy how attracted he was to me. Then just maybe he would forget that I had proposed he design a tattoo for me that I didn't even want.

"No problem," he said, glancing at me.

His eyes didn't even linger for half a second. He reached into his bag and pulled a sketch pad and some pencils out, placing them on the table.

I slumped and cleared my throat. I was throwing my

best stuff at this guy and he was all business.

"So, what were you thinking?" he asked, placing his coffee aside so he could open the book. "A flower? An animal of some kind?"

Okay, think, Layla. If you just throw him a bone and keep him talking, maybe you can get to know each other a little bit.

"Actually, I was thinking of maybe a butterfly?" I said, taking a shot in the dark.

"Really?" he asked with a note of skepticism.

Oops. Misfire. "You don't like butterflies?" I said.

"No. They're fine," he replied. "They're just a little, I don't know, juvenile, I guess."

I blinked and stared down at my coffee. Had Drew just called me *juvenile*?

"Oh, but hey. Maybe I could do something with it," he said quickly.

"That's all right. I'm open to other ideas," I said, trying to sound sophisticated to erase that whole *juvenile* impression from his mind. "What are your thoughts?"

In other words, what's *your* impression of me?

"Well. I was thinking . . . I don't know, you're clearly a free spirit—"

Bingo! He *did* get me.

"But earthy, too," he added.

Or not. I glanced down at my cute tweed gauchos and the hot four-inch heeled designer boots I loved so much. My mother was earthy. I, however, prided myself on being *funky*.

"You think I'm earthy?" I asked.

"What about a rose of Sharon?" he said.

"A rose of Sharon," I repeated, confused.

"It's beautiful and untamed and it grows in all these unexpected places," he said.

Okay. Beautiful, untamed, unexpected. Those were good. I took a sip of my coffee and tried to look thoughtful. "That could be something."

"Hang on," he said, pulling his sketch book to him.

He worked for a few minutes while I watched, completely transfixed. An incredibly intense expression came over his face and he hardly blinked the whole time he was sketching. A lock of his long hair fell over his face and he flicked it away and continued to draw. Damn he was sexy.

"What about something like this?" he asked, holding the book up. In five minutes he had drawn an incredibly intricate and gorgeous flower.

A flower that he was going to have somebody scratch onto my person with a needle.

I put my coffee down, feeling suddenly nauseous.

"You don't like it," he said.

"No! It's not that. It's just—"

"This wouldn't be the final design," he said quickly. "It's just to give you an idea."

"Oh. Well, okay." As long as we weren't going to Vinny's right now. "It's really pretty."

Drew smiled and my heart stopped beating. He didn't do that very often so when he did, it was that much more stunning.

"Good. I'll work on it some more tonight," he said, closing the book. "You have no idea how much this is going to help me, Layla. Crabbe wanted me to do some more designs before he'd hire me for sure, but if I tell him someone specifically requested me, it'll definitely tip the scales."

I gulped. Never in the last few week had he strung so many words together at once. Clearly he was really psyched about this. What had I gotten myself into?

"Cool," I said tremulously.

Drew put all his tools away and I relaxed a tad now that everything tattoo-related was out of my sight. Still, I had to come up with another topic of conversation before he bolted again like he had tried to do last night. "So, did you talk to the woman from the gallery this morning?"

"Yeah. She said she sold another of my pieces after we left," Drew told me.

"That's great!" I said, touching his arm. "Maybe you won't ever need the tattoo work if you keep selling your pieces."

I hope, I hope, I hope.

Drew gave a laugh that made me feel like a naïve five-year-old. "It's not like it's enough to pay the bills," he said. "Most artists need to do something else on the side."

"Oh," I said, disappointed. "Well, it's still amazing."

"I know. Maybe you're my good luck charm," Drew said, looking into my eyes and sending chills down my spine.

Good luck charm? That was more like it. Maybe he *had*

just been nervous the night before. Already this date was going far better than that one had. Good thing I had come up with my tattoo idea so that I could see him again.

Now if I could only figure out a way to get out of it.

By the time Drew pulled into my driveway an hour later, I was clinging to his jacket for dear life. Not because he'd been driving crazily or anything, but because I was so tense.

After chatting with him all afternoon, I still didn't know where I stood. Was he going to kiss me or not? If he did, would it be a deep, searching kiss like the one in the tattoo parlor, or a dismissive forehead kiss like the one outside the garage?

And what could I say to get myself out of our little tattoo arrangement without him hating me? After all, now he was counting on my business to help him land the design gig.

Drew stopped the bike and I swung my leg around, my knees quaking. I took off my helmet and put it on the rack. This time, much to my glee, Drew killed the engine and removed his helmet. But he didn't make a move to get off his bike.

Huh.

"So," he said.

I took a deep breath.

Okay, so he was gorgeous. Okay, so he was the standard against whom all other boys had been measured for the last two years. But that didn't mean I couldn't be as direct with

214

him as I would be with any other guy.

Right?

Come on, Layla. Stop being such a wuss.

"Hey, Drew?" I said, stepping close to him. "There's something I've been meaning to ask you all day."

Before I could say another word, he wrapped one arm around my waist and pulled me close. My heart jumped into overdrive. He was about to kiss me, and if my racing pulse was any indication it would *not* be a little peck on the forehead.

"What's that?" he asked

There was no going back now. "Okay, I was wondering—"

"Sweetie! There you are!" my mom shouted from the doorway. "I was hoping you'd be home soon. Dinner's all ready!"

Drew's arm dropped from my waist and he pulled back sharply, nearly knocking his bike off balance.

I turned around, my face burning bright red.

"Hi, Mom," I said through my teeth. "Be there in a minute."

My mom grinned knowingly at me. She *knew* she was being embarrassing.

Great, Mom. Way to have your fun at the exact wrong moment.

"Okay!" she sang before going back inside.

"Sorry about that," I said to Drew. When I turned around again, he had already put his helmet back on.

Guess I wasn't getting kissed after all.

"I gotta go," he said quickly. "We'll talk more about the tattoo later."

"Oh, uh . . . okay," I said.

No! I wanted to scream. *I don't want to talk about the freakin' tattoo! I want to find out if you like me!*

But before I could even think of one semi-normal thing to say, Drew pulled away, leaving me with my unasked question burning in my throat.

"You guys! What am I going to do?" I wailed on Monday morning as Cara, Anna, and I stood in front of the bathroom mirror.

"I'm still processing the fact that you're dating Drew Sullivan," Anna said, stunned. "*The* Drew Sullivan."

See? He's totally famous.

"Yeah, but maybe not for long. I mean, not only do I still not know what the deal is between us, there's the minor issue of the tattoo. When he finds out I don't really want it, after all the work he's put into it, he's going to totally hate me."

"That is quite possible," Cara said, applying her lip balm.

"Cara!" I cried, whacking her arm.

"Ow! Layla, come on," she said with a laugh. "You know what you have to do. Stop torturing yourself and tell him the truth."

"That I asked him to design me a tattoo just so I could get a second date? That I like him so much I was willing to risk having my skin scarred for life just so I could hang out with him?" I slumped back against the sink next to her. "I can't do that. It's too humiliating."

"Then you'll just have to suck it up and get the tattoo," Anna said.

"Ha-ha."

"Look, Anna's right," Cara said. "It's either confess or go under the needle. Sorry to be so blunt, but you're the one who's always saying she values the truth. And it doesn't get more honest than that."

Groaning, I covered my face with my hands. They were right. Of course they were right. I couldn't go out and mar my body for life just because I was too scared to tell a guy how much I liked him.

The door to the bathroom opened and I lifted my head. Debra Jack and Hannah DeSalvo. Just what I needed.

Instantly, Anna shrunk back against the wall, trying to disappear. Debra had really messed with that girl's head.

"What's the matter *Miss Most Likely To*?" Debra asked, sauntering over to the mirror. "Upset because Nate dumped you?"

Wow. Could anything be farther from my mind just then?

"Actually, Debra, you might want to get your stories straight," I said, pushing myself away from the sink. "*I* dumped *him*."

Debra and Hannah both laughed. "Yeah, right. Like I'm gonna believe the town ho."

Her words stung, but I kept my expression impassive. I

glanced at Anna, whose face had reddened with anger on my behalf.

"At least I'm not a cold, heartless bitch who only feels good about herself when she's tearing other people down," I said to Debra.

Hannah instantly laughed and Debra's jaw dropped wide open.

"See? Even your friends know it's true," I said. Then I grabbed my book bag and strutted out of the room with Cara and Anna in tow.

"Omigod, Layla, that was awesome," Anna said once we were out in the hallway. "I've always wished I could do that."

"Hey. I promised you would be there," I told her. "I'm just sorry I didn't also dunk her head in that gross toilet, too."

"That may have been a little extreme," Cara said. "You *are* a lady, after all."

"Yes, I am," I said, batting my lashes. "That did feel good though."

On the other side of the bathroom door we could hear Debra tearing into Hannah for laughing at my joke. We giggled and moved out of the line of fire.

"But you know what? I don't even care about her or that stupid website," I said with a smile. "None of that really matters anymore. I just want to get this thing with Drew over with."

"Yeah? You're going to tell him how you feel?" Cara asked.

"I am," I said, hoping that if I sounded confident I would somehow *become* confident.

I was just going to have to bite the bullet and tell him how I felt. . . .

And just hope he didn't laugh in my face.

Drew

fourteen

That afternoon I was supposed to meet Drew at Vinny's to look at his finished design. Instead I was going to burst his bubble and tell him I didn't want the tattoo after all.

I was. I was. I *really* was.

Or at least that was what I kept telling myself as I approached the front door. I grasped the handle, took a deep breath, and steeled myself. One way or another I was about to find out how Drew Sullivan really felt about me.

I rounded my shoulders and strode into the shop.

"Hey. Drew's girl," the burly man behind the counter said, looking up from his magazine. "How's it going?"

I smiled. *Drew's girl*. That had such a nice ring to it.

"Fine," I said, with more confidence than I felt. "Is Drew here?"

"He's in the back with Tom. They're working on Nicole," he said.

My entire body prickled with heat. Nicole? Who the heck was Nicole?

Don't overreact until you have all the information, a little voice in my mind warned. Oddly, it sounded a lot like Cara.

"Oh, right. Nicole," I said blithely. "Guess I'll just wait then."

I strolled casually around the shop, pretending to check out the tattoo designs on the wall. The buzz of the needle sounded from behind one of the curtains and I edged toward it. As I got closer, I heard Tom's voice.

"Not much longer," he said. "You're doing great. This is a tough girl you got here, Drew."

My heart slammed into my rib cage. What? If he had a tough girl in there, then what was *I* doing out *here*?

"I know it," Drew said proudly.

"Hey. I wouldn't be doing this well if you weren't here," a girl's voice said. A kind of husky, older girl's voice.

"Aw. You two are too cute," Tom joked.

My stomach turned over and I placed my hand against it. My palm touched my navel piercing and I almost hurled. I'd gotten that for *him*. I'd let Tom slam a hole in my belly button for a guy who was right behind that curtain with too-cute, too-tough Nicole.

"Oh, ow!" Nicole said. "Drew! Hold my hand."

Oh, man. What a drama queen!

But wait. Hadn't I done exactly the same thing when I'd

gotten my piercing? Hadn't I grabbed the hand of exactly the same guy?

I had to see what this girl looked like. I just had to. If she was my double or something, then Drew was going right into the sicko hall of fame.

Ever so carefully I stepped toward the curtain and peaked around the side. There, laying on her side on the table with her hip exposed to Tom, was a Playboy-worthy blonde with a spray-on tan and claw-like blue nails. Her eyes were squeezed closed and she was clutching the hand of the man of my dreams. And breaking his fingers from the look of it.

Okay, not my double. But if that was his type, then he was *so* not interested in me.

"Hey! You can't go back there while they're working!" Burly man said suddenly, scaring me right out of my skin.

I jumped back, letting the curtain fall closed. The buzzing stopped and instantly I turned and sprinted out of there as fast as my high heels could carry me. There was no way I was going to let Drew catch me spying on his girl-friend's tattooing with tears in my eyes. No way in hell.

That night I was on the phone with Cara, relating the whole awful story, when another call interrupted us. I checked my caller ID and my breath caught.

"It's him," I told her. "What is he calling me for? To tor-ture me?"

"Talk to him and call me right back," she said.

"Okay. Wish me luck," I said.

"Luck!" she sang.

I clicked over and sat down on the edge of my bed.

"Hello?" I said, trying to sound all calm.

"Hey, Layla! What happened to you today?" He sounded totally and completely normal. My heart was going spastic.

"I couldn't make it," I said flatly.

"Oh. Donny said you were there but you bolted," Drew said.

Donny. Burly man. I was going to kill that sucker. If I ever had an army behind me.

"Well, I wasn't feeling well," I told him.

No need for him to know I'd seen his Pamela Anderson-esque girlfriend.

"Oh. Sorry," he said. "Wanna try again tomorrow?"

"Actually, Drew," I said, sort of irritated at his clueless-ness. "I don't think I want to get a tattoo anymore."

It was amazing how much easier that was to say now that I knew he was otherwise engaged. With a bombshell.

"Oh. Why?" he asked.

"I just kind of decided it's not my thing," I said curtly.

I wanted to be done with this. I felt like a total idiot. I'd been chasing some guy I'd never stood a chance with in the first place. Now I remembered why I didn't like to chase guys.

Let them come to you. Always let them come to you. Drew hadn't done that once. And when we were together, he was always so hot and cold. Maybe because he felt guilty about cheating on his girl.

"Oh. Okay, then," he said. "So I guess I'll . . . see you around?"

"Yeah, see you," I said.

And I quickly hung up the phone.

The week passed in a haze of self-pity. Normally that is not my style, but this time, I couldn't help it. Clearly I was incapable of making good decisions. I'd dumped Nate and turned Ian down, and for what? For nothing.

Even on Wednesday afternoon when the vice principal called me into his office and told me he was taking down the Kensington Daze, I couldn't muster so much as one iota of self-righteous indignance at having the paper's autonomy stripped away.

Yeah. It was that bad.

By the time Friday finally arrived I was exhausted and sad and just wanted to sit in my room and eat an entire package of Double Stuf Oreos. Of course I would have to smuggle them past my mother. She was not a fan of additives or preservatives.

I was just settling into bed with my iPod and my contraband cookies when my phone rang. I jammed the package of Oreos under my pillow just in case my mom walked in, and picked up.

"Hey, Cara," I sighed.

"Hey, Mopey," she said. "Get dressed. Mike and I are picking you up in fifteen minutes."

"For what?" I asked.

"We're going to that party at Alex Smith's house," she

said. "And snapping you out of this zombie-like state of yours is going to be the theme of the night."

"Gee. That sounds appealing."

"How's this for appealing? If you're not ready when we get there, I'm going to let Mike dress you," she said.

I grimaced. Mike may have been a nice guy, but he could have also been a contestant on *Beauty and the Geek*. I knew Cara was bluffing, but I had to appreciate the effort.

"All right," I said reluctantly. "I'll be waiting outside."

Alex's party was a rager. People were hanging out on the front lawn, on the porch, in the upstairs bedrooms. Clearly this was not a parentally attended, or sanctioned, thing.

"How long before the cops bust this shindig?" I asked as we trudged up the front steps, sidestepping someone's spilled beer.

"I give it half an hour," Cara said. "Have fun while you can."

We walked through the door and were instantly greeted by Alex's older brother Rick, who had graduated two years ahead of us. He was bare-chested with a plaid shirt tied around his head like a turban.

"Greetings! Welcome to my flunk party!" he shouted, waving a beer around.

"Flunk party?" I repeated.

"Yes!" he said, then burped. "I flunked out of college, so now, we party!"

Then he turned around and whooped, earning a round of cheers from the partiers in the dining room, who appeared to be playing strip poker.

"Wow. Sounds like my kind of party," Mike joked. He was, after all, our valedictorian.

"This is *Rick's* party?" I said, my pulse starting to jump around. Rick had graduated the same year as Drew. Chances were . . .

"He's not necessarily going to be here," Cara said, reading my mind. She placed her hands on my shoulders and steered me toward the kitchen. "Your assignment for the night is to go talk to some new people. In half an hour I am going to come find you and I want you to have met at least three new people. Guys or girls. I don't care. Just have fun."

"Yes, sergeant," I said, catching sight of some cute guys hanging out by the kitchen sink. I gave her a little salute and headed over there. Of course the moment I stepped into the brightly lit room, I heard a very familiar voice say my name.

"Layla."

I turned around, heart in my throat. Yep. There he was. Drew Sullivan. Standing next to the refrigerator in a tight black T-shirt, holding a beer, looking hotter than ever.

Damn Cara.

"Oh, hey, Drew," I said casually, trying not to look directly into those unbelievable hazel eyes.

"How've you been?" he asked.

As if you care. As if you, like, missed me this week or something while you were cuddling up next to your bunny-of-the-month.

"Good," I replied. "I've been . . . good."

God playing it cool was tough. My heart was pounding in my ears and my palms were sweating like crazy. Clearly I liked this guy. I liked him so much I couldn't even control my bodily functions around him. And was I insane, or was he looking at me like maybe he liked me a little bit, too?

"Drew, I—"

And then I saw her. Nicole. She walked into the kitchen behind Drew and every male jaw in the room dropped. May as well have been Angelina Jolie striding through the door. She was wearing a slinky black top and a denim miniskirt that could have passed as a belt. Her eyes fell on me and Drew and she made a beeline for us.

"I gotta go," I said.

Then I turned and fled.

I seemed to be doing that a lot lately.

Half an hour later, the cops had yet to do their job and I couldn't find Cara and Mike anywhere. I retreated to the basement and found an empty stool at the old-school wooden bar. All around me people chatted and laughed, couples sucked face, a few people danced to the music being pumped throughout the house. Everyone was having fun but me. All I wanted to do was go home and get back to my Oreos.

"Hey, Layla."

Tony Aames, a guy from my Trig class, attempted to sit down next to me and missed the stool. He righted himself, laughed, then handed me a red cup full of liquid. "I brought this for you."

"What's in it?" I asked, sniffing the drink.

"Rum and Coke," he said a bit blearily. "I saw you sitting here by yourself, and I thought you might be thirsty, so I got you some."

"Thanks," I said, taking a sip. Might as well have *some* fun at this party.

"You're welcome," Tony said with a smile. "You know, I always thought you were really pretty. Even in kindergarten. 'Member I asked you to be my girlfriend?"

I looked at Tony and laughed. "No."

"Well I did," he said.

"What did I say?" I asked.

"You said maybe," he replied. "But I think you meant no."

"Oh. Sorry about that," I said, gulping down some more of my drink. It was fizzy and sweet and I liked it.

"S'okay," he said, patting my back.

I laughed and looked at Tony out of the corner of my eye. Maybe it was the rum and Coke doing the thinking, but he was actually sort of cute. Although I had to admit that his purple and green geometric-print shirt left much to be desired.

"Want another one?" he offered, gesturing at my now-empty cup.

"Definitely. Thanks," I agreed.

Why should I let Drew Sullivan and his bimbo girlfriend spoil my good time? I was going to relax and have some fun if it killed me. And Tony seemed harmless enough.

When he returned with another cup, I drank it down quickly. It was much stronger than the first and chugging it was the only way to get it down.

"Thanks. This is exactly what I needed," I told him. My head was already starting to get fuzzy.

"Yeah, it is," he said. "Why don't we go sit on the couch? I'll get you another one."

"Okay," I said, thinking the couch sounded like a good idea in my hazy state. "Let's go."

While Tony mixed another drink at the bar I walked over toward the wall and dropped down on the old vinyl couch, a foot or two away from Darren Rourke and Missy Tyler, who were going at it like they were auditioning for porn. When Tony sat down next to me, his leg was pressed into mine. I took a sip of my drink and edged away, but I was right near the arm of the couch and there wasn't far to go.

"You know, I always thought you were pretty," Tony said.

"You said that already," I told him with a laugh.

"Oh."

He smiled, then, out of nowhere, leaned in and kissed me. I was so surprised, I dropped my drink on the floor and it splattered all over my legs and skirt. For a split second I tried to kiss him back—a reflex—but then I felt how gropey his lips were and smelled his rancid breath and my stomach turned.

I wasn't sure if it was the liquor or because he was practically giving me a tonsillectomy right there in the middle of a party, but I was definitely going to be sick.

"Tony," I said, shoving him away.

"What? Whatsa matter?" he slurred.

"Oh, God," I said.

fifteen

The next thing I knew, I awoke in a dark room. My head felt like it weighed four thousand pounds and something was ringing. Loudly.

I turned over onto my side and saw my bag lying on an unfamiliar floor. The ringing persisted. I grabbed the strap and pulled my bag onto my stomach, then groped inside for my cell phone. When I lifted my head to answer the call, my brain felt like it was spinning.

"Ohhhh." I groaned, dropping down again.

I brought my phone to my ear. Only one way to make the awful ringing stop. I answered it.

"Hello?"

"Layla! Thank God. Where are you?" my mother asked.

Good question.

"Cara's house?" I replied, taking a stab in the dark. I slowly sat up, enduring the shots of pain that attacked my skull, and looked around. I was lying on a couch in someone's living room, but it was so dark, I couldn't tell whose living room it was.

"Was that a question or a statement?" my mom asked loudly.

I squeezed my eyes closed against the pain. Her voice had never sounded so shrill.

"A statement," I told her. "I'm fine. I'm going to stay over, if that's okay."

"Okay," she said. "But next time, try to remember to call me?"

"I will, Mom, I promise," I said, just trying to end the call. "See you tomorrow."

I hung up the phone and squinted into the darkness, trying to get my bearings. Was I fine? I wasn't sure. I mean, how could a person be fine when they didn't know where the hell they were?

My mouth was dry, and my head pounded. Everything kept spinning. Then I remembered the multiple cups of rum and Coke. . . .

Panic washed over me suddenly. Tony. Oh, God. This wasn't Tony's place, was it?

A key turned in a lock, and the door opened. Blinding light flooded the room from the hallway outside. "Who's there?" I demanded.

A lamp snapped on and I blinked against the searing pain from the light. When I was finally able to focus, it took me half a second to recognize who was standing over me.

"Drew?"

"Hey. You okay?" he asked. He pulled a bottle of soda out of the paper bag he was holding and handed it to me. "Drink this. It will help settle your stomach."

"Stomach?" I echoed.

He chuckled and sat down on the coffee table next to me. "Do you remember anything about the party?"

The party. Right. And Tony. I had puked all over Tony. Oh, God. Had Drew *seen* that?

"It's okay," he said. "Happens to the best of us."

I was mortified. Drew Sullivan had seen me puke. He had seen me *puke*! Why, why, why hadn't I just stayed home? Stupid Cara.

"What time is it?" I asked, placing the soda aside and digging in my bag for a breath mint. I found one and popped it in my mouth. Instantly the dry sourness melted away. Small relief.

Drew glanced over his shoulder at the clock in the small kitchen at the front of the apartment. "Three A.M."

"How did I get here?"

"Me and Nicole drove you," he said. "You don't remember any of this? You were still awake when we got you to her car."

"Nicole?" I said. My face flushed with humiliation. Not only had I vomited all over some guy in front of Drew, but he and his girlfriend had saved me? Could this get any worse?

"Yeah. In fact, we should probably keep our voices down," he said, whispering now. He glanced over his other shoulder where I noticed, for the first time, the open door to the bedroom. "She's kind of a light sleeper."

Great. Just great. Drew's bodacious girlfriend was asleep in the next room and I was out here all woozy and gross. This was unacceptable.

"Okay," I said, pushing myself up off the couch. Bile rose up in my throat, but I held it back. I had to get out of here. I picked up my bag and started for the door. "I gotta go."

"Uh, how, exactly?" Drew asked.

I stopped. He had a point.

"I'll . . . uh . . . take the bus," I said.

"At three A.M.?" Drew said, standing. "Layla, don't be stupid. Just stay."

He got up and put an arm around me. Instantly, I ducked out of his grasp. Drew blew a sigh through his nose.

"What's wrong?" he asked.

"What's wrong?" I whispered, whirling on him.

Oops, big mistake. It took a second for the room to catch up with me and I almost swooned.

Drew reached out and grabbed my arm. Much to my chagrin, I found myself leaning into him. I took a deep breath and steadied myself. I stood on my own and looked him in the eye.

"What's wrong is *that*," I said, lifting my arm toward his bedroom and the snoozing blonde. "Haven't you ever heard the expression 'three is a crowd'?"

Drew's brow knit. "What?"

234

I blew out a sigh of frustration. "She is not gonna want me here in the morning," I said.

"Oh, she won't care. She crashes here all the time. She doesn't care if I have friends over. When you come from a big family, you get used to having lots of people around all the time."

Now my head was really spinning.

"Who comes from a big family, you or her?" I asked, confused.

"We come from the same family," he said. "Layla, Nicole's my sister. You know that, right?"

"Your *sister*?" I said.

"Yeah. She's a few years older than me," he said. Then he took a step back and looked at me as if I had just sprung a third nostril. "Wait a sec. You thought she and I were . . . *together*?" Drew's voice cracked on that last word.

"Uh . . . yeah," I said.

"Okay. That's gross," he said.

Suddenly I felt like the biggest moron ever to walk the earth. My mind was already going over all the things I'd overheard at the tattoo parlor. I had completely misread all of it. They were brother and sister. They were *brother* and *sister*!

Drew laughed. "Layla, everybody knows she's my sister!"

"Well, I didn't," I practically wailed.

Drew smiled and shook his head at me. "That's why you bolted from Vinny's on Monday, isn't it? You thought Nicole was my girlfriend."

I was snagged. I was so very snagged.

"Kind of?" I said with a wince.

"Layla, why didn't you just ask me?" he said kindly.

Another good question. People were just full of those tonight. "Because . . . well . . . because . . ."

Because I'm an idiot who's been in love with you for two years and I'm too nervous around you to deal?

"Oh, God," I said, sitting down on the couch. I placed my head in my hands for a moment, steeling myself for my confession. Drew stood in front of me, his arms crossed over his chest. "Drew, the thing is, I *really* like you," I said finally, looking him in the eye. "In fact, the only reason I said I wanted the tattoo was so I could spend more time with you."

Slowly, Drew smiled. "That's sweet," he said.

"It is?"

He came over and sat down next to me. "Misguided, but sweet," he told me. He took a deep breath and let it out audibly. "I really like you, too, Layla."

My heart did about a thousand backflips. "You do?"

"You're surprised?"

"It's kind of hard to tell sometimes," I said.

"Well, I do. I just don't know what to do about it," he said. "I mean, you're so young and everything, I—"

"So young," I interrupted. "What do you mean, so young?"

Drew blinked. "Well, you're fifteen, right? I mean, five years from now the age difference might be fine, but right now—"

"I'm not fifteen," I said quickly, cutting him off. "I'm eighteen."

"What?" Now it was Drew's turn to be confused.

"Where did you get the idea that I was fifteen?" I asked.

"From Mrs. Haley at Kensington High," he said. "I take sculpture classes with her at the community college and she said—"

"Drew, Mrs. Haley is senile," I said. "I haven't had a class with her in two years. She probably *thinks* I'm still a sophomore."

"Oh, my God," Drew said with a laugh. He covered his mouth with his hands and looked at me, embarrassed. "You're eighteen?"

"Yes!" I squealed, then slapped my hand over *my* mouth and looked at the bedroom. No wonder he'd been so hot and cold with me. He thought that every time he kissed me he was committing a felony. "Looks like we were both misinformed."

"Well, I was misinformed. You just jumped to conclusions," Drew said.

"Semantics," I told him with a smile.

"Wow. Eighteen is way better," Drew said, looking me in the eye. "Now I don't have to feel guilty about thinking about you so much."

"You've been thinking about me?" I asked, inching closer to him on the couch.

He nodded. "A lot."

My heart jumped wildly in my chest. "Really?"

"I have to show you something."

Drew got up from the couch and crossed the room to an easel covered with a cloth. He hesitated a moment, almost as if he was reconsidering. Then with a quick yank, he pulled the cloth away.

It was a drawing of me.

I completely stopped breathing. Somehow I pushed myself off the couch and went to look at it up close. I could hardly believe my eyes. In the drawing I was sitting in the middle of a field of wildflowers, glancing over one shoulder and laughing. My hair was long and wavy and flowing. I was holding a messy bouquet of blooms from a rose of Sharon.

There was something so relaxed and honest about it.

"I hope you don't think I'm a stalker or something," he said.

I cracked up laughing. If only he knew . . .

"Actually, I think it's beautiful," I murmured, truly overwhelmed.

"That's how I see you," he said softly.

I gazed up at him. "So, now that we've cleared everything up, can you do me a favor?"

"Anything," he said, his eyes twinkling.

"Kiss me, and don't even think about feeling guilty about it."

And he did. A soft, slow, amazing kiss that went on and on and on, but still felt as though it ended much too soon.

"I've wanted to do that for such a long time," he whispered, still holding me close.

Leaning my head against Drew's chest, I realized it was the kiss that I'd been hoping for, too. And there was no doubt in my mind that this kiss was the beginning of something warm and safe and very, very special.

The End

The Choice Redux

So, was it worth it for me to take a risk like that? You tell me. Of course, if you're not happy about it, you can go back to page 103 and try again. But only if you really, really want to!

Here's a sneak peek at

Hook Up or Break Up #3

Lose Yourself

As I drove home from Trent's, I sang along to the radio at the top of my lungs. All sorts of emotions were swirling around inside of me. One minute I was giddy, thinking of Trent's kiss. The next I was depressed and, for some reason, guilt-ridden, thinking of Zach and questioning whether I had ever loved him. How could I betray three years of absolute certainty with him by doubting it now? Then seconds later, I'd be hopeful and happy again. I was going from smiling and laughing and singing, to almost crying and choking on the lyrics, to smiling again, in seconds flat.

If anyone had seen me they definitely would have called a psych ward.

So you can imagine what my heart did when I pulled onto my street and saw Zach's Xterra parked at the curb in front of my house. I nearly drove right off the road and into Mrs. Splete's rhododendrons.

What the hell is he doing here? I thought, somehow managing to pull my car into the driveway and *not* slam into the rear bumper of my mom's Saab.

I stared out the window. Zach was just standing up from the doorstep. He looked, of course, drop-dead gorgeous, and he was wearing the blue ribbed sweater I'd given him for his birthday.

Okay, just be strong. Whatever he has to say, do not *get emotional. Don't give him the satisfaction.*

I opened the car door and paused. My legs were shaking.

"Hey," he said, pushing his hands into the front pockets of his jeans. He actually looked tentative. My confident, cocky boyfriend looked tentative.

Ex-boyfriend.

"Hi." I managed to get up and closed the car door behind me.

"Where're you coming from?" he asked, glancing at my car.

Unbelievable. Keeping tabs on me? "Why are you here?" I asked him.

"Noelle, I'm so sorry," he said, taking a few steps toward me on the front walk. "I didn't mean for any of this to happen. I was never remotely interested in Melanie, okay? It was all just . . . stupid."

Wow. On a sincerity scale of one to ten, this apology was headed directly for the two-hundred range.

"I love you *so* much Noelle," he continued. "I don't know what I was thinking."

He was right in front of me now and he looked even better close up. He'd let a little stubble grow out on his chin which he *knew* was the sexiest thing in the world. He reached out and took my hand gently in his.

"Let's just forget this ever happened, okay?" he said, ducking down to look into my eyes. "We'll go to the prom together like we were supposed to. Everything can go back to normal."

Normal. God, I loved the sound of that. Normalcy was my thing. Normalcy, familiarity, predictability. I looked up into Zach's hazel eyes as I had done a million times before, and felt myself start to cave. It would feel so good just to fall into those arms. The arms that had belonged to me for three straight years. What had I been thinking when I doubted I'd ever loved him? This was my Zach. Yeah, maybe he'd said some harsh things to me, but I'd said harsh things to him. And he was practically begging here. That couldn't have been easy for him and his macho-man ego.

But do you really want to deal with that ego again? I asked myself. Especially when I had Trent—sweet, attentive Trent—who actually listened to me and respected my opinions? Trent, whose incredibly intense kiss was still lingering on my lips?

"Whaddaya say?" Zach asked, lifting my hand and entwining our fingers together with a smile. "Be my girl again?"

Part of me wanted to say yes. Yes, yes, yes. But when I thought about all the heart-wrenching pain of the past couple of weeks, I hesitated. And Zach saw it. He knew me that well.

"What?" he said warily, his face falling.

"It's just . . . I'm kind of seeing someone," I said, biting my lip. "You know . . . Trent Davis?"

Zach dropped my hand and took a step back. The expression on his face was pure revulsion. "You're gonna throw away three years for that *junior*?" he spat. "What does that *sop* have that I don't have?"

In that moment, everything inside of me shut down. Zach couldn't have done a better job of exhibiting his faults if he tried. He was so condescending sometimes, so judgmental. And such a sore, sore loser.

Everyone has their flaws, of course. It wasn't as if I hadn't known about Zach's forever. But now I didn't *have* to deal with them anymore.

"I'm sorry, Zach. It's . . . I'm going to have to think about this," I told him.

Zach took a breath. For a split second I was sure he was going to shout at me and I braced myself, but instead he shook his head and looked at the ground.

"If that's what you need," he said finally. "You know where to find me."

I sighed. "Thank you," I told him. I started past him, but paused. "And for the record, I'm really sorry for those things I said to you at the party that night."

Zach looked up at me. In the entire time we were together, I had never seen him look so vulnerable. "Me, too,

Noelle. Really sorry," he said.

"Thanks."

Then I turned and walked into my house, a little dizzy, a lot drained, and more confused than ever.